"Mugino…"

Former underling member of Item
Shiage Hamazura

A Certain Magical Index

22

KAZUMA KAMACHI

ILLUSTRATION BY
KIYOTAKA HAIMURA

The Star of Bethlehem

A supermassive floating fortress created
according to the plans of Fiamma of the
Right, who belongs to a shadowy Roman
Orthodox organization. Made from a patchwork of materials
drawn from Roman Church religious facilities throughout the
world, its completed form floats at an altitude of ten thousand
meters and spans a radius of over forty kilometers. Inside the fortress,
in addition to the ritual site at the very front that controls the Star, there are
monorails, various containers that function as storehouses, and facilities that serve
as bases for manual administration and operation. A spell deploys a unique field
around the Star of Bethlehem, creating an atmosphere identical to that of the surface, even at
the fortress's high altitude. Though originally designed to be operated by a great number of sorcerers,
it can operate automatically as well. This fortress is complete as long as Fiamma is present.

"I wonder if we'll make it, says Misaka, sighing and cheering you on. Do your bessst. Sigh, when will I be able to meet that person?"

Sister entrusted to an Academy City affiliate in Russia
Misaka number 10777

c o n t e n t s

VOLUME 22

KAZUMA KAMACHI
ILLUSTRATION BY: KIYOTAKA HAIMURA

NEW YORK

A CERTAIN MAGICAL INDEX, Volume 22
KAZUMA KAMACHI

Translation by Andrew Prowse
Cover art by Kiyotaka Haimura

TOARU MAJYUTSU NO INDEX Vol.22
©Kazuma Kamachi 2010
Edited by Dengeki Bunko
First published in Japan in 2010 by KADOKAWA CORPORATION, Tokyo.
English translation rights arranged with KADOKAWA CORPORATION, Tokyo,
through Tuttle-Mori Agency, Inc., Tokyo.

English translation © 2020 by Yen Press, LLC

Yen On
150 West 30th Street, 19th Floor
New York, NY 10001

Visit us at yenpress.com
facebook.com/yenpress
twitter.com/yenpress
yenpress.tumblr.com
instagram.com/yenpress

First Yen On Edition: March 2020

Yen On is an imprint of Yen Press, LLC.
The Yen On name and logo are trademarks of Yen Press, LLC.

Library of Congress Cataloging-in-Publication Data

Names: Kamachi, Kazuma, author. | Haimura, Kiyotaka, 1973– illustrator. | Prowse, Andrew (Andrew R.), translator. | Hinton, Yoshito, translator.
Title: A certain magical index / Kazuma Kamachi ; illustration by Kiyotaka Haimura.
Other titles: To aru majyutsu no index. (Light novel). English
Description: First Yen On edition. | New York : Yen On, 2014–
Identifiers: LCCN 2014031047 (print) | ISBN 9780316339124 (v. 1 : pbk.) |
   ISBN 9780316259422 (v. 2 : pbk.) | ISBN 9780316340540 (v. 3 : pbk.) |
   ISBN 9780316340564 (v. 4 : pbk.) | ISBN 9780316340595 (v. 5 : pbk.) |
   ISBN 9780316340601 (v. 6 : pbk.) | ISBN 9780316272230 (v. 7 : pbk.) |
   ISBN 9780316359924 (v. 8 : pbk.) | ISBN 9780316359962 (v. 9 : pbk.) |
   ISBN 9780316359986 (v. 10 : pbk.) | ISBN 9780316360005 (v. 11 : pbk.) |
   ISBN 9780316360029 (v. 12 : pbk.) | ISBN 9780316442671 (v. 13 : pbk.) |
   ISBN 9780316442701 (v. 14 : pbk.) | ISBN 9780316442725 (v. 15 : pbk.) |
   ISBN 9780316442749 (v. 16 : pbk.) | ISBN 9780316474542 (v. 17 : pbk.) |
   ISBN 9780316474566 (v. 18 : pbk.) | ISBN 9781975357566 (v. 19 : pbk.) |
   ISBN 9781975331245 (v. 20 : pbk.) | ISBN 9781975331269 (v. 21 : pbk.) |
   ISBN 9781975331283 (v. 22 : pbk.)
Subjects: CYAC: Magic—Fiction. | Ability—Fiction. | Nuns—Fiction. | Japan—Fiction. | Science fiction. | BISAC: FICTION / Fantasy / General. | FICTION / Science Fiction / Adventure.
Classification: LCC PZ7.1.K215 Ce 2014 | DDC [Fic]—dc23
LC record available at https://lccn.loc.gov/2014031047

ISBNs: 978-1-9753-3128-3 (paperback)
        978-1-9753-3129-0 (ebook)

10 9 8 7 6 5 4 3 2 1

LSC-C

Printed in the United States of America

BATTLE REPORT

Fiamma of the Right.

The project he'd been planning had finally started in earnest.

To start with, he'd gathered all the necessary pieces from the Roman Orthodox Church's holdings all around the world and then built the fortress his ritual needed.

Scooped up onto this battleship as it rose, Touma Kamijou heard the voice of his fated enemy.

"I welcome you—to my fortress, the Star of Bethlehem."

The mobile stronghold wasn't the only threat, however. Fiamma had another trump card yet to be played:

"Sally forth, Archangel Gabriel, the POWER OF GOD. Blow them all to bits."

Having reached a field hospital in the Elizalina Alliance of Independent Nations, Shiage Hamazura received help from the sorceress Elizalina, who successfully eliminated as much of the ill effects from the Crystals eating away at Rikou Takitsubo's body as she could.

But then Hamazura and Takitsubo read a document sent to the Alliance called the Kremlin Report, quickly learning that Russian forces were preparing to carry out a special operation: a procedure for defending nuclear launch facilities by using biological weapons—and the location where they planned to execute this inhumane plan was very close to the settlement where Digurv and the others lived.

"I couldn't talk much while we were in the settlement, but I remember everything those people did for me. I want to fight for their sake, too."

Meanwhile, Accelerator had been sojourning in the Elizalina Alliance of Independent Nations as well, but even Elizalina's cleansing technique hadn't granted him a way to save Last Order.

Accelerator ultimately decided that if he wanted to save her, he had no choice but to decipher the mysterious parchment after all.

Moments later, Elizalina yelled a warning at him:

"Run away!! They'll be here soon. If they mount a serious attack, our forces won't be enough to stop them! Their goal is the parchment you're carrying!!"

An archangel's ferocious attacks may have been assailing Russia's skies, but the term *angel* didn't refer only to Misha Kreutzev.

There was another.

Hyouka Kazakiri, born from scientific technology and AIM dispersion fields, was challenging the angel of water:

"...If that is the reason you would harm my precious friends, then I'll use all the power I can muster to stop you."

Another battle was unfolding in another place as well.

In the Vatican, Matthew Reese, who had decided to abandon his very position as the pope of Rome and to fight once more as a simple Crossist, was confronting Cardinal Peter Iogdis:

"Do you understand? We are fighting so you can survive. Promise me you will not die before this war ends."

In a Russian palace, Bishop Nikolai Tolstoj trembled with rage, having been completely left out of the plan.

"Send in the reserves...I want that fortress blown up!! Right now!!"

*　　*　　*

And Mikoto Misaka, newly arrived in Russia, was listening to a Sister as she relayed details about the movements of an independent Russian unit.

"*Nu-AD1967. They are preparing to fire an old Soviet strategic nuclear warhead, reports Misaka, summarizing the details.*"

A myriad of battles were unfolding in multiple places.

Unbeknownst to these fighters, a great deal of people had gathered to defeat the archangel Misha Kreutzev.

Accelerator had intervened between Misha and Kazakiri.

Acqua of the Back had attempted to reduce the archangel's power by redirecting the telesma comprising Misha's body into himself based on their mutual control of the element of water.

Touma Kamijou had tried to damage the archangel by destroying the ritual site on the Star of Bethlehem.

And as a result...

"*...You think it'll go that easy? You don't have Misha anymore. I still don't know why things went so well, but humans managed to beat an archangel. No matter how you think about it, the scales are tipping in our favor.*"

But it wasn't over.

Even after the enormous loss of an archangel, Fiamma's mental state didn't waver as he confronted Kamijou atop the Star of Bethlehem.

"Misha Kreutzev's role ended when it changed these skies into night. I'd like to say phase one is now complete, but even now, I've gotten a little bonus."

Two right arms were on the verge of clashing.

But before they did, Fiamma of the Right said only this:

"*One can only fully wield true power in a true world...It's time I showed you exactly what that means.*"

CHAPTER 9

Moment of the Great Distortion's Correction
Broken_Right_Hand.

1

Shizuri Mugino.

The fourth-ranked Level Five. A bona fide monster who could freely use her terrifying ability Meltdown. And a fated rival that Hamazura had thus far defeated not once, but twice. Appearing before him now—he, who had fled Academy City to faraway Russia—was a hunting dog. It was no exaggeration to say she was one of the most infamous of her kind.

As far as Hamazura knew, she'd lost one of her arms. Looking carefully, he saw that her yellow coat sleeve seemed strangely baggy. Maybe it was only her wrist that had a human form and the inside was something more robotic.

"Pfeh."

There were no words.

All Hamazura noticed was Mugino hanging her head, shoulders moving up and down eerily, mechanically.

"Heh-heh-heh. Ku-ha-ha-ha-ha-ha-ha-ha-ha-ha-ha-ha-ha!!"

"...!!"

When she looked up, she was sticking her tongue out.

On its tender red flesh rested a small case. A rectangular holder, the kind you might put mechanical pencil lead into. It contained some white powder. Something Hamazura knew all too well.

Crystals.

This stuff had tortured Rikou Takitsubo. It was almost like a drug, allowing users to intentionally cause their abilities to go berserk. Hamazura's and Takitsubo's wanderings in Russia were merely one part of their efforts to combat its side effects—and yet, Mugino had dug up the root of all their struggles just to throw it in their faces once again.

She must not have even thought about it…

…about the wall that divided a Level 0 from a Level 5.

Come to think of it, where *had* Takitsubo gone? Was she truly safe? Nobody was doing anything terrible to her, were they?

Hamazura spat out the words as they boiled up in his mind. "After all this time, you *still* want to use that shit on Takitsubo?! Just to make us suffer a little bit longer, just to hurt us a little bit more, without any logical reason?!?!"

In response to his fury, Mugino gave him a scornful grin.

Her mouth moved.

But she didn't answer. After all, she hadn't opened her mouth to speak.

Ker-crack.

Shizuri Mugino's upper and lower teeth crushed the case of Crystals between them.

Hamazura's eyes trembled; he couldn't believe what he was seeing.

Meanwhile, the soft *crick-crack-crunch-crunch* noise continued. There was no mistaking that it was coming from Mugino's mouth—the sound of her breaking down and chewing the case's sharp fragments. Human mouths, of course, were not the sturdiest things. The taste of blood was probably filling her mouth at that very moment.

And yet.

Only that plastered-on smile remained in the monster's expression.

"…Takitsubo, eh? Why should I care about every little thing that small fry does…?"

*Mrmph-mmph-hmrph...*Mugino continued to mutter as the sounds of fibers tearing filtered through her mouth.

Something was filling her.

Something nondescript began to circulate through the body of the woman named Shizuri Mugino.

"Crystals...A substance that allows espers to intentionally cause their abilities to go out of control. Some researcher from that crew Rescue, or whatever they call it, said it was the path to Level Six. Even ignoring the hopeless answer from the Tree Diagram, they struggled in vain, using resonance or telepathy or something like that. Clearly the Crystals still have their secrets, but I don't think about stuff that complicated."

Shiage Hamazura had misunderstood.

Misunderstood how serious it was that he'd defeated the fourth-ranked Level Five twice. And now that he stood on the same stage as the powerful, he finally began to realize what lengths they would go to for the sake of eliminating the powerless Level Zero.

"Hey, Hamazura? If the fourth-ranked Level Five went so crazy she couldn't control herself, how much worse do you think the damage would be?"

Whoosh!!!!!!

A bloodcurdling white light erupted.

Not one light, not two.

Thousands, tens of thousands of intense lights radiated out from the woman named Shizuri Mugino, in every direction.

2

Touma Kamijou and Fiamma of the Right.

These two men confronted each other atop the Star of Bethlehem.

An intense bloodlust filled the air, emanating from Fiamma and flooding the space around him. An abnormal power had gathered to his third arm, the symbol of his strength. It was so overwhelming even Kamijou, who knew little about the inner workings of sorcery, could easily grasp its presence.

Kamijou had no choice but to face this terrible opponent alone. The sorceress Lesser wasn't on the Star of Bethlehem. Sasha Kreutzev, who had been present only moments ago, had fallen through the cracks in the floor Fiamma had destroyed, dropping down to the fortress's lower levels. Kamijou had nobody to call on.

But he never faltered.

He clenched his fist into a tight ball as he faced his enemy.

A Soul Arm rested in Fiamma's hand. It was controlling Index remotely, granting him access to the knowledge in her 103,000 grimoires.

It was so close, Kamijou might reach it if he simply stretched out his hand.

But the sheer wall of strength named Fiamma made that nigh impossible. This wasn't a problem that could be easily solved by just charging in blindly, and he knew that.

Slowly, slowly…As Kamijou gauged the distance, little by little…

Fiamma smiled.

It was a sign of his cold, merciless heart.

And yet, it was also the expression of a person who believed he wasn't doing anything malicious whatsoever.

"The Star of Bethlehem has risen. My control over celestial bodies using Gabriel has also been completed. Each of the four planetary aspects has returned to its rightful position."

Shoom went the sound of something cutting through the air.

Fiamma had casually swung his third arm; it was glowing faintly.

"Everything is now prepared. It's past time for me to have that right arm of yours. Once I use it as a medium to wield the power that has taken root within me, Project Bethlehem will be complete."

"…You would go that far to see the Roman Orthodox Church win?" Kamijou tightened his right fist.

Fiamma shook his head. "I don't care about the Roman Church. Well, I would be lying if I said I wasn't thinking about Crossist society in a broader sense. But fundamentally, my actions are for my own benefit." He spoke smoothly, without a single pause. "And to add to that, I am *not* the cause of this war."

It wasn't a prepared sermon. He hadn't simply memorized some set phrases. These were the fundamental ideals that utterly permeated the man named Fiamma. That was why his speech lacked even a moment's hesitation.

"Yes, I may have pulled the trigger, but the rage, resentment, and envy underpinning this war—that vortex of negative emotions—is simply something that has *always* inhabited the hearts of people all around the world. Otherwise, could any amount of violence incite a war that spread the flames of conflict so quickly?"

Fiamma's voice was the only thing flowing between them.

"I am their indulgence."

"..."

"Say I didn't really want to do this, that someone else had ordered me to. Make an excuse like that to yourself, and you can commit even the worst atrocities. Humanity is an ugly species."

"And you think that's supposed to justify everything you've done?"

"Not at all. And I don't think that way, either," Fiamma explained simply. "I had two objectives with World War III. The first was to collect every bit of the supplies and data I needed for my plan under the pretext that they were war necessities. And the second was to conduct the ritual to lure the enemy I need to defeat into the open."

His third arm.

The "symbol" that made him special flickered with light, strong to weak, pulsing.

"After all, even if you acquire a sword that can slay the king of demons, you can't defeat it if the incarnation of evil is nowhere to be found."

A moment later.
A slash came.

An attack coming directly from the side.

Distance didn't matter. And it couldn't fit within this one room anyway. The giant *thing* that appeared pierced the walls in its path—and in that instant, the entire room was torn apart, the result-ing cut shaving off a massive piece from the Star of Bethlehem itself.

Ba-boom!! The roar reverberated a moment later.

There was an almost electric flash.

Kamijou's right hand couldn't cancel it all. If he'd tried to take it head-on, the force would have carried his body away, blasting it thousands of meters back, possibly even sending him hurtling down to the surface.

However.

"Oh?"

A smile from Fiamma.

Touma Kamijou was still standing in the cloven room. Knowing he couldn't nullify the impossibly massive attack, he'd struck out at the sidelong hit with an uppercut from directly below. As a result, Fiamma's attack had veered slightly upward, scraping right over Kamijou's head.

In other words:

"You not only erase—you've learned to parry as well, have you?" Fiamma asked, sounding impressed.

And then:

The next attack that came was one nobody present could have anticipated.

Neither Kamijou nor Fiamma.

It was someone else.

In the skies spread past the broken ceiling, something blinked.

A white light.

A moment after Kamijou realized this, a gigantic pillar of pure-white light rained straight down onto Fiamma, bathing his entire body.

Ssszzzzhhhhhhhhhhhh!! A second later, Kamijou heard a sound like oil popping in a hot pot.

"What...?!"

Everything exploded.

The light was blinding, like a welding flame, and before he knew it, Kamijou was covering his face with his hands. The flash actually gave him a headache—and then his feet were in the air. A moment later, his body careened several meters backward.

This was only the aftermath. The intense heat caused the air to explode, and simply being exposed to the shock wave had sent a single human body flying.

But...

"An optical weapon of Academy City?"

A cool voice could be heard beyond the explosive flashing lights.

The very man supposedly under fire by the mystery attack hadn't changed his tone in the slightest.

"Officially, they claim to have four satellites...But now, as I thought, the map of space territory seems to have major discrepancies. It's very likely they have smaller satellites and spaceships deployed around a giant station."

The ray of pure-white light that had fallen from overhead should have been digging into the top of Fiamma's shoulders.

But it wasn't.

Instead, the third arm coming out of his shoulder was raised straight upward, acting like a huge parasol. It blocked the downpour of light from encroaching upon Fiamma's space. And then, he casually swung his right hand. That was all.

And yet.

Boom!!!!!! The air rumbled.

Blown and scattered by the third arm, the white light shot away like a tiny eraser flicked by a finger. With no more than that, the irradiation of immense light, which had brandished such enormous power, vanished. Kamijou's vision was nothing unusual for the average human, so he obviously couldn't observe what was happening outside the planet's atmosphere. But he knew. Fiamma, the man before him, had just shot down a whole satellite with a flick of the wrist.

"It's nothing to be surprised about." Fiamma of the Right's third arm slowly drifted. "In fact, I'm ashamed I had to expose my half-formed appendage like this."

"You..."

"I thought I'd displayed this in the Elizalina Alliance of Independent Nations already. My right arm does whatever I need it to, always providing the optimal output to match whatever challenge or difficulty I encounter. It doesn't matter if what I'm facing is an optical weapon or anything else. Naturally, nothing can compete with *me*."

This is insane, Kamijou sputtered.

This was way beyond holding back in rock-paper-scissors until just after you saw what the opponent threw. Fiamma was basically claiming to be all-powerful. Kamijou could throw out rock, paper, or scissors—but as long as Fiamma put out his hand, he'd simply win no matter what. It didn't matter what shape he had his five fingers in. The moment he challenged somebody, he'd win.

That was why Fiamma didn't need to worry about things that were normally important.

Speed.

Hardness.

Intelligence.

Muscle strength.

Distance.

Manpower.

Weaponry.

For someone who could end the battle by putting out his hand, trivial things like slowly building up to a victory, searching for the primary factor for winning, or thoroughly preparing beforehand. He only needed to do one thing to win: swing his right arm. That was it. Before, he seemed to have had a limit on how much he could use it, but he'd apparently overcome that as well by bolstering it with Index's knowledge. As he was now, Fiamma could obtain as many victories as he desired.

Maybe they'd only be personal victories and not political victories. That was probably why he'd needed the Roman and Russian Churches. But in this situation, he held far too great an advantage.

How was anyone supposed to fight an opponent like him?

Finding a way to climb onto the same stage that Fiamma stood on and finding a way to achieve certain victory against him were two entirely different problems.

"Nevertheless, you should be proud."

Fiamma, with his aberrant right arm, spoke cheerfully.

Not that he was enjoying his battle with Kamijou.

He was merely enjoying the simple fact that what he desired was within his grasp.

"I should have expected as much of the right hand I have such high hopes for. My right arm seems to be unsure how much power to use against that fist of yours."

Boom!!

It was a horizontal swipe.

Naturally, Kamijou's right arm wouldn't block it. Fiamma's arm wasn't built so shoddily. Kamijou stuck his right arm out in front of him. Just as he was about to touch the tip of Fiamma's third arm, he veered his fist away, as if to slide along the man's forearm. His own body slid to the side to follow that momentum.

The tension that gripped his entire body was so intense that it almost seemed like it would shorten his life span.

Perhaps Kamijou's hand should have also been considered abberant for being able to compete against a right arm like Fiamma's.

"...!!"

Still, despite all his efforts, Kamijou couldn't counterattack properly. Fiamma's body had already disappeared.

His opponent couldn't move up or down, but he could move across as much horizontal distance as he wanted. After instantly retreating three kilometers back, Fiamma landed on the roof of another building on the floating Bethlehem.

At the same time, he launched his next attack.

A light burst out—from the remote-control Soul Arm in his hand.

"Warning. Chapter 22, Verse 1. Commencing spell Eli Eli Lama Sabachthani— Full activation in seven seconds."

Rrrrrm!!!!!! A bloodred flash surged forth in a roar.

A magic circle had appeared in front of Fiamma, and a pillar of light had leaped out of it, shooting straight at the distant Kamijou.

Something ran up Kamijou's spine.

He couldn't have remembered this as a memory, but something like an instinct was intensely rejecting this.

"...?!"

He immediately thrust out his right hand, but what came was pressure heavy enough to break his fingers.

He couldn't drive it all away.

This...guy...!! Kamijou clenched his teeth. *He doesn't rely only on his right arm?! It's got so much packed into it, and you're telling me it's still nothing but a crude, incomplete item to him?!*

And then...

"As I thought, simple spells have their limits."

That line came from directly behind him.

He didn't have time to turn around to meet the voice. Fiamma was already there, his third arm gripping a giant sword made of light. He swung it horizontally, aiming for Kamijou's neck.

Kamijou's Imagine Breaker was weak to attacks coming from multiple directions at once.

It would be too difficult to cancel both at once, and at this level of power, even if he stuck with one and faced it head-on, he'd be crushed.

But Kamijou didn't have the time to hesitate.

Even now, the bloodred light ray was threatening to squash his body while the great sword was approaching from behind to chop off his head.

"Ooohhhhhhhhhhhhhh!!" he shouted, keeping his right hand thrust forward while pivoting his body around.

He positioned himself so that his leg was underneath his right hand and at a right angle to the light ray of the spell Eli Eli Lama Sabachthani.

And then he pulled his right hand back from the ray.

Rather than taking it head-on, he changed his positioning to only subtly graze the ray's edge.

A moment later.

Crack!! The red beam's trajectory was forcibly twisted.

It was like in bowling, when throwing the ball purposely away from the center of the pins to come in from the side. Its path bent, the light ray flowed behind Kamijou, parried diagonally.

Yes.

Toward Fiamma, who was trying to take his head off.

Got y—

Kamijou turned around at the sound of the explosion, but his eyes went wide before he could confirm the result.

Fiamma of the Right had ignored the light approaching him and continued with his third arm's horizontal swipe. The sword of light blasted the red ray into oblivion with a single hit, then tore through the air, still heading for Kamijou's body.

He didn't have time to get his right hand in position.

He also didn't have room to dodge with footwork.

"!!"

Without hesitation, Kamijou dropped to the floor as though his legs had been swept out from under him. An instant later, the sword passed right over his head. He knew it was already slicing brutally through the fortress's walls; the rumbling noise hit his body like another shock wave.

Fiamma smiled thinly.

With his sword drawn all the way to the end of its swing, he toyed with the remote-control Soul Arm.

"…Continuous attacks from a distance are less precise. I suppose I knew that based on what happened in Elizalina's country."

The remote-control Soul Arm gave off an unnatural light, pale and red.

"Warning. Chapter 29, Verse 33. Crimson Stone of Pexjarva— Full activation in seven seconds."

Wha…?!

Blindsided, Kamijou immediately got ready to make his next move, pushing the soles of his shoes into the floor as he tried to get up.

A moment later.

Crack-crack-crack!! A strange, intense pain shot up Kamijou's toes and through his ankles, shins, and knees. It was almost as bad as if his bones' joints had been wrenched out of place. It felt like something he couldn't see had made its way up from the floor, through his feet, and into his body.

"Kuh…gaaaaaaaaaaaaaaaaaaahhhhhhhhhhhhhhhhhhh!!"

Kamijou slammed his balled fists into his thighs.

The moment his hand made contact, the intense pain stemming from his legs suddenly vanished.

He got onto his knees, but Fiamma didn't stop there.

"Warning. Chapter 35, Verse 18. A Rain of Sulfur Shall Scorch the Earth— Full activation in five seconds."

Arrow-like objects, blazing orange, rained down.

And more than just a couple.

Almost fifty arrows appeared close to the roof before falling upon Kamijou like a suspended ceiling.

…He has his own skills as God's Right Seat and he's pulling one thing after another out of Index's knowledge…?!

Still on the floor, Kamijou clenched his teeth, then swung his right arm.

Several of the arrows turned into orange sparks and blew apart in a spray of color. Their fine particles continued, crashing into the swarm of the rest of the arrows still trailing their target, causing a fruitless explosion in midair.

But he couldn't knock them all down.

Orange arrows plunged straight past the young man's body, brutally crushing the stone floor. Even as he was pelted by sharp fragments, Kamijou rolled backward, then stood up on two feet.

Touma Kamijou and Fiamma of the Right.

They glared at each other through the white smoke between them.

"Ah, this is no good. Even though I couldn't have rehearsed a situation like that, it's still important to pay attention to the theory's margin of error. Anything less is simply rude when the enemy I need to defeat is standing right before me."

Now that both the room and the fortress had been cut in two, a cliffside into the skies appeared right under Kamijou's feet.

Beyond the sheer fissure, he could see white clouds and the Russian earth that had been upturned.

In a situation where one wrong step would lead to a deadly jump from almost ten thousand meters up, neither Fiamma nor Kamijou took their eyes away from the other's face.

The movement of Fiamma's limbs didn't quite possess the speeds of Kanzaki or Acqua. They were a normal person's normal movements, same as Kamijou. Nevertheless, mountains had been shattered, and the ground had been ripped apart. The inconsistency was rather bizarre.

Though fully aware of that terror, Touma Kamijou found his lips moving. "Enemy you need to defeat?"

"Well, of course. I'm not being overly dramatic, mind you. And I don't want to take over the world, or wipe out humanity, or anything of the sort. If anything, that sort of change is the furthest thing from what I'm working toward. My goal is to keep the right things moving in the right direction."

The remark was clearly at odds with his words and actions thus far.

But the words that followed brought his ominousness to the fore.

"This world is distorted."

One short sentence.

Casual words—but they conveyed Fiamma's thoughts keenly enough to send a shiver down his spine.

"Whether it be the four aspects that I mentioned before or the immense, sordid negative energy fueling World War III—everything is hopelessly distorted. The causes are numerous. All kinds of problems are cropping up everywhere. Almost as if the world itself is growing decrepit, and its joints are weakening. The one we call God has created a perfect system and arranged the cogs so that everything would spin correctly. Why, then, did things distort so easily? …The answer is simple. Several of those cogs have reached their limit."

That was why he would put it back to normal.

Put it in words, and it was a simple goal.

But considering how many he'd sacrificed against their will before now, it was easy to see how *wrong* his process was.

"Cogs need to be exchanged, and in certain places, it's very likely new mechanisms will have to be set up. Think of it as having to do internal rewiring when renovating an old house. In a way, the malice manifested by World War III was merely getting some clogged dust out."

Fiamma spoke about these things in a tone that made it seem like they weren't important to him.

"After washing off all the dirt on the cogs, I'll reapply the lubricant— Crossist codes—and restore their original smooth motions. I think that should work as a decent analogy. I think it would be more prudent to compare it to Noah's ark...Although, even after washing the world away with the great flood, it seems that clinging malice remained even in the post-flood world."

"...Lubricant," murmured Kamijou, glaring at Fiamma's face. "Are you talking about using a spell or something that will rewrite people's minds in a way that's convenient for *you*, like the Croce di Pietro during the Daihasei Festival?"

"It's not that complicated. I only need to teach the masses a lesson; that's the easiest way for people to learn. Think about it—if I were to swing my completed arm just once, every last person would have no choice but to realize the difference in power whether they wanted to know or not...Now, I wonder how afraid humanity will have to be before they come to terms with reality. The reality that what I'm doing is the same as the punishments of legend, like raining thunderbolts atop the heads of those who go against the codes. The reality that I can offer salvation to people throughout the world as long as they obey those codes. The reality that when the Star of Bethlehem first began to glitter in the night sky, a new age had already begun."

In the end, was Fiamma of the Right a Crossist?

Or was his belief that the cogs God had created were distorted and that he could "fix" them the greatest blasphemy?

That wasn't what Kamijou was interested in, though.

"Offer salvation to people throughout the world..."

Fiamma would cover the world with happiness, but only in the scope *he* could imagine.

He would never acknowledge any other values.

A world like that...

It *would* be a utopia, in a certain sense.

A planet where all but happiness had been obliterated.

"Have you ever really gone out *into the world* and seen every last bit of it for yourself? Seen how many people are smiling?"

"Hmm. Your opinion is quite fascinating." Fiamma grinned. "But I'll consider it *after* I've saved the world."

A moment later:

A giant sword suddenly rose, from straight beneath him to straight above him.

It dug right up under Kamijou's right armpit, heading immediately for his right shoulder.

He had no time to evade, nor room to parry.

Thmp.

With an unbelievably soft noise, Touma Kamijou's right arm came off at the shoulder.

3

Accelerator had successfully brought down the angel of water.

Despite having manipulated vectors, his breath was ragged, and his two feet on the snow trembled madly with exhaustion.

He'd kept the water angel's detonation as small as he could. For now, he'd protected hundreds of kilometers of Russia that the explosion would have obliterated—as well as the people living there. He'd made a difference.

And yet.

Accelerator thought his heart would stop.

Because, in front of him—

Crashed into a wall of snow was a single car. It was the one Misaka Worst had been driving, the one Last Order had been riding in. It was clearly not fine. The hood was massively dented, and the front windshield had shattered.

The surrounding trees had all been mowed down in the same direction.

This was the aftermath of his battle.

Last Order and Misaka Worst had taken the brunt of its shock wave.

"..."

Accelerator's weary body seemed ready to crack and sink into the snow.

As things stood, he wondered what had he even been fighting for.

Both Misaka Worst and Last Order lay limp inside the car, no doubt having sustained severe injuries—Last Order especially. Aiwass's influence had already bound her from within, and now she'd been injured from without. Just imagining the peril her body faced was terrifying.

Is there anything I can do?

He still didn't know how to use the parchment. Meanwhile, the war was intensifying with no end in sight. On top of that, a string of battles had taken its toll on both Last Order and Misaka Worst. Would Last Order physically hold on until he could find his so-called clue, and it guided him to a concrete solution?

"...You might...be able to do something..."

Then he heard a voice saying that.

A woman's weakened voice.

"You have someone you want to save with your own hands as well, don't you? I'm not exactly human, but I can understand human feelings like that."

Cornered, turning around with excessive hostility in his eyes, Accelerator then spotted the angel of science. Her body had turned strangely translucent.

"Maybe I can entrust my goal to a person like that as well. I've used too much of myself. It won't cause my existence to disappear, but I probably won't be able to affect the outer world for a time."

"What are you talking about? What do you mean, I might be able to do something?!"

"September thirtieth."

The two words the angel of science spoke made Accelerator's eyes go wide.

The day Amata Kihara had kidnapped Last Order. That date held a special relevance, even when taking in his whole life.

"My friend, named Index...She removed the virus in that girl's head by singing a particular song to her."

And then, Index.

The one keyword both Aiwass and that Level Zero had mentioned.

That piece of information was something he could no longer ignore. Accelerator's attention turned to the angel of science, as though he were being drawn in.

And yet.

Like the flame on a guttering candle, that angel of science's features grew more and more indistinct.

"......The 'song's' contents...entered rest within girl's virus as well as my linked mind. Because the original...one corresponded...to 'me,' it may not...work...on that monster...derived...from me...but if you...overwrite...the song's...parameters..."

A song? The theory where you can control someone's mental state through sensory stimulation? Just like how I fought against Amai's virus, I'd affect her brain directly...

Vanishing.

Not enough time.

No time to have her teach him this so-called song from start to finish.

"...You'll...be okay..."

The angel of science put an index finger to her temple.

Even that fingertip had mostly disappeared.

"The treat...ment re...corded the song...in her...hea—"

Her weakhearted smile, too, blurred.

"The para…meters…too…you already…know—"

She vanished.

There was nothing left to see.

No voice lingered, either, or anything else audible.

"…"

Accelerator flicked his electrode switch and checked the vectors nearby. The AIM dispersion fields filling the space like they did in Academy City were completely gone. The angel of science had "disappeared"…or maybe she'd been forced to "go home" to Academy City.

He thought just for a moment, then called out to the broken-down parked car's driver's seat—to the limp Misaka Worst.

"…You alive?"

"Unfortunately. For a while, Misaka figured she'd pretend she was dead to make it easier."

The girl poked her head up, and with surprisingly nimble motions, extracted herself from the crushed driver's seat and came out onto the snow.

Without particularly caring, Accelerator noted to himself, "Then you heard all that."

"Data on the song used to erase the virus is still in Last Order's memory region," answered Misaka Worst in a "whatever" tone. "Maybe she meant it would help cure her if you extracted it. Oh—Academy City's number one can even steal other people's memories by reading the vectors of electrical signals in their brains? Wow, amazing."

"…My vector manipulation ability only extracts whether there is an electrical signal or there isn't—a sequence of zeroes and ones. It can't play back what kind of memories they're actually connected to. It's not like you've ever met someone who could look at the surface of a CD and imagine the music on it, right? Same thing."

"Then what'll you do?"

"I'll use your power," said Accelerator without skipping a beat. "You're one of the Sisters series, too—you should be able to directly access a certain massive information source called the Misaka network."

"Last Order is the highest of us. Misaka only has normal access privileges. She can't look into the command tower's mind. If she could, the angel would have controlled her to make her attack you."

"You don't need to get inside the kid. She's got this habit where she shares her memories with the other Sisters to make backups. Meaning, if you can reach the other Sisters through the network, chances are good you'll be able to get the song data."

"Not very prudent. If Misaka matches her timing with the command center's tower, she'll have a chance to bury some evil data in her."

"Yeah. But generally, I think people call that imprudence *trust*," spat Accelerator. "Thanks to that, I think I might have barely found a way."

"Keh-keh. But even if Misaka found the song, wasn't the problem that you couldn't use it as is? Where are you gonna get the extra parameters you need to change its contents?"

"I got it."

Accelerator reached into his pocket.

The parchment.

Something he couldn't explain with science.

However.

Couldn't he say the same about the monster Aiwass in Academy City? No matter how much that thing was based on AIM dispersion fields, could he really call it *scientific*? He'd defeated Accelerator, supposedly number one, so easily—if he thought of Aiwass as an existence outside their rule set, it would actually make a lot more sense.

In which case...

"I might find the parameters if I search this thing. Academy City—and the other form of technology outside it. If I put them together, I might find a path leading to a solution."

4

Shizuri Mugino "burst."

She had fired a cannonade of white lights rocketing out from her in every direction.

The eerily dark sky and the unnatural four-toned paths glittering in it—this supernatural phenomenon was completely upstaged by the overwhelming flood of light. Just as nighttime cityscapes blotted out the stars, Shizuri Mugino's power reigned across this Russian land, a symbol of negative science.

The raging emissions eventually converged toward a single point. It was an arm. An erect construct almost twenty meters tall. Just as Hamazura looked upon it in dread, the arm of flashing light dove at him from above like a collapsing building.

"…???!!!"

In haste, he rolled to the side.

The Meltdown arm explosively incinerated both the thick layer of snow and the ground beneath it.

The blast had been powerful enough to throw a fully grown man over ten meters away. Hamazura's mouth was frozen from fear in a shouting gesture.

He suddenly realized he'd lost a ton of moisture.

Forcing his stuck-together throat to move and taking in a breath, Hamazura set his mind to work.

The attack hadn't hit him directly. If it had, he'd already be in pieces.

A water vapor explosion…!!

His entire upper body was giving off a stinging pain. His whole spine creaked. But he didn't have time to complain about it.

The next attack was coming.

The only good thing, perhaps, was that Mugino, who had gone berserk of her own accord, couldn't take careful aim in her current state.

The difference between the good and bad, however, was too great.

Shizuri Mugino was no longer visible.

Her flashing arm unraveled, and again, thousands, if not tens of thousands, of beams shot out from her whole body in every direction. It was not an instantaneous event, like a saber in a robot anime, but rather a perpetual, continuous emission. The brightness blotted out even the contours of the body of the woman named Mugino.

The incredible mad dance of light burned afterimages into Hamazura's vision, which ceased to function properly.

In that flashing vortex that would induce sharp headaches after a single glimpse, he decided to hit the deck for the moment. The fact that Mugino's attack, which could instantly liquefy even steel, hadn't managed to cleave his body in two yet was nothing short of a miracle.

He couldn't get close like this. Any attempt would unequivocally mean death.

Mugino's Meltdown had been overwhelming in their previous battles, too. After all, she could fire attacks at will that could pierce someone's body even after passing through a myriad of obstacles. Simply breathing loud enough to be heard was the same as dying. That was what Hamazura was facing.

But something was different.

More so than everything else.

At this point, Mugino was the same as a blast furnace or the sun. Holding his breath and approaching from a blind spot or taking advantage of a psychological opening to attack—chances like that were no longer possible. This was an all-too-massive light. An iota of carelessness in the approach would mean fatal wounds for a human body. And it wasn't up for debate what would happen if he *touched* it.

Plus:

"…Haaamazuraaa…"

In the explosive din, Hamazura still heard the husky voice. He could tell that voice was coming closer. Yes—*closer*. Shizuri Mugino, who had "burst" with such force, was slowly coming his way. A blast furnace, hot enough to roast flesh just by being nearby, was walking toward him. She was truly an angel of death now.

This was the significance of the Crystals.

This was Meltdown.

Her ability had been demonically strong to begin with. What would happen if she added a "drug" that would bring out even more destructive power? Shizuri Mugino showed him exactly what that would look like after becoming this world's hell.

"...Look at all I've sacrificed."

She sounded nightmarish.

With only her voice, she seized the insignificant man's heart.

"I knew what would happen if I used the Crystals. It wasn't hard to imagine. But I did the right thing. I made the sacrifice, Hamazura. I paid the price to stand here. It wouldn't be right if you were left unharmed...You don't think you can settle things without giving something up, do you...?"

Was she even human like him?

That was Hamazura's honest impression. At this point, he didn't retain even a fragment of the vague resentment he felt toward powerful espers during his time in Skillout. Now he was certain that people like this were insane. The world they lived in was in another dimension. It was supposed to be a game of chicken, competing for distance to the cliff—but Shizuri Mugino had simply flapped the wings on her back and easily flown off it. Against a monster like that, no matter how far he drove, the only thing waiting for him would be a straight drop off the cliffside.

He couldn't win.

He couldn't do anything.

Still on his hands and knees in the snow, Hamazura couldn't make a move.

Even if he pulled his assault rifle's trigger now and shot every bullet he had, what good would it do against a monster like that? She showed no opening. No blind spot. What the hell was he supposed to do to leave a scratch on a Level Five continuously firing killer beams in 360 degree arcs?

"...Hamazura..."

Death was calling his name.

Death was coming for him.

"Hamazura."

No point in showing his back. If he tried to flee on foot in this snow, Mugino only had to focus a little and fire to end it all. Similarly, if he tried to hide in the trees, she'd blast him and the trunk together in one blow.

Even if he ran far away, he'd be killed.

But even so, standing to face her would only shorten his life.

But then…

What the hell am I supposed to do…???!!!

"Haamazuraaaaaaaaaaaaaaaaaaaaaaaaaaaaaaaaaaaaaaaaaaaaaaaa
aaaaaaaaaaaaaaaaaaaaaaaaaaaaaaaaaaaaaaaaaaaaaaaaaaaaaaaaaaaaaa
aaaaaaaaaaaaaaaaaaaaaaaaaaaaaaaaaaaaaaaaaaaaaaaaaaaaaaaaaa!!!!!!"

A roar.

All that white painting over his field of vision immediately vanished. Or—no; that wasn't right. Fired in every direction, the attacks were now concentrating on a single point—to pierce Shiage Hamazura head-on. To precisely open a giant hole in their target's torso—that and nothing else.

At this point, it didn't matter where he fled.

An attack of certain death that would cut through any obstacles.

I'm…de—?!

His breath caught, but his hands still sprang up. Without checking if the safety was even off, he pointed the assault rifle's muzzle at Mugino. To create a possibility where Rikou Takitsubo would survive, even if it was a 1 percent chance, or a 0.1 percent chance, Hamazura tried to pull the trigger.

And then.

Shizuri Mugino's roar began to spread out explosively.

"Aaaaaaaaaaaaaaaaaaaaaaaaaaaaaaaaaaaaaaaaaaahhhhhhhhhhhhhhhh
hhhhhhhhhhhhhhhhhhhhhhhhhhhhhhhhhhhhhhhhhhhhhhhhhhhhhhhhhhhh
hhhhhhhhhhhhhhhhhhhhhhhh!!"

Suddenly, all light vanished.

And then, Shizuri Mugino's body stumbled and collapsed into the snow.

"Huh…?"

The scene before his eyes was incomprehensible.

Hamazura hadn't pulled the trigger yet. Nor had a third party abruptly appeared and attacked Mugino. Nobody had done anything.

And yet, Mugino had lost her power on her own before dropping like a marionette with severed strings.

He didn't have the presence of mind to think about why.

...Am I...saved...?

That was all he could think.

Until he noticed something.

Specifically, how Shizuri Mugino's body, sunken in the snow, was trembling. Her face, with the special makeup peeled off, had burst into a huge amount of sweat, a strange sight in ultra-cold Russia. She looked like she had come down with a high fever. Hamazura knew what was happening. He knew, because a girl he had watched over so closely had been in a very similar state.

It was the Crystals.

They had originally been developed to purposely cause espers to go out of control. Because some could bring out more power when berserk, a few espers like Takitsubo had been provided with Crystals, but they'd never been suitable for espers who didn't have the affinity for it.

Shizuri Mugino never had that kind of special compatibility.

The Crystals had steadily eaten away at Takitsubo's body, and she was someone who *had* the innate compatibility required to use them with any semblance of control. It didn't need to be said how terrible the effects would be if Mugino used it without heeding the danger.

Those were the lengths that Shizuri Mugino had gone to.

Her power as number four wasn't enough anymore. If it was guaranteed that she could kill Shiage Hamazura, whom she'd lost to twice, she didn't care what happened to her body afterward. That was probably what she'd been thinking when she'd used the Crystals.

...Even just standing must have been absolute hell for Mugino.

Of course, didn't Hamazura, a Level Zero, understand this well?

If there was something that would raise a person's strength so easily, without any risk, nobody would have any difficulty.

"...Why...?"

Something squirmed and writhed in the snow, calling out in desperation.

It was what remained of the queen who had once led an organization called Item.

"Why, damn it? Fuck, fuck, fuck!!!!!! The Crystals...What happened to the Crystals? Just a little more...Just ten more seconds, and I could have cleaned everything up...!!"

"..."

Now fully aware of the situation, Hamazura's hand trembled. The assault rifle's muzzle wavered indecisively. He had a clear line of sight to Mugino, who was still writhing in the snow.

He could kill her now.

If he killed her, she'd never come after him or Takitsubo again.

The index finger on the trigger twitched.

However.

Was it truly okay to kill her?

Who was it, exactly, who regretted having a death match with Shizuri Mugino after meeting her again, just before coming to Russia?

Hamazura looked at the fallen Mugino again.

He remembered her being the most attractive member of the mostly all-girl Item team. Her fashion sense wasn't bad, either, from what he could recall. Her limbs were long and slender, and all of her mannerisms overflowed with elegance. Hamazura, who had been treated as nothing more than a two-bit lackey, had never heard anything about her, least of all her personal history. Even so, he'd still been able to guess that Mugino was a high-class young lady from somewhere.

And yet.

"Hamazuraaaaaaaaaaaaaaaaaaaa!! Don't look down on me, you bastard! I'll kill you...I'll kill you with my own two hands, I swear to you!! I screwed everything up back then. Ever since you shot me in that ethanol plant!! If I don't crush you, I'll never get it out of my mind!!"

Even now, Mugino was in tatters. She'd lost an arm as well as an eye. Her face had a severe burn on it. And he couldn't begin to tell what her insides must have looked like. Were her organs still where they should be? Did she even have the right number of them? Nothing strange had been added in there, had it? He didn't even know that. How much had happened while Hamazura wasn't watching? Considering how grievous her wounds were, the very fact that she could keep getting up, again and again, was abnormal. He couldn't even imagine how much grotesque technology had been put into her to make that possible.

And on top of all that, the Crystals.

Mugino was a shadow of her former self. Her body no longer contained the spirit it once did. She looked as if a light poke with a fingertip on her skin was all it would take to for it to sink into a thick, rotten jelly. It was stranger that she had been able to stand right up until a few moments ago. Academy City's "darkness" had made her into a perfectly disposable tool.

...I wonder why I had to turn into such a horrid monster.

Hadn't Shizuri Mugino said that in District 23? And what had *he* thought when he heard those words? When he broke out of Academy City, didn't he decide he was done with these back-alley death matches?

"Mugino..."

If he killed her now, would anything have changed?

Hadn't he come to Russia because he didn't want to shed any more of the blood for the machinations of Academy City's darkness?

"Muginoooooooooooooooooooooooooooooooooooooooooooooooooo ooooooo!!"

The next thing he knew, he had run over to her. He tossed his assault rifle to the side. He didn't need something like that. Not for this.

No attacks came from Mugino, who had stood in his way as such a formidable obstacle until now. She simply continued to shake.

Hamazura approached her, squatted, put his arm around her back, and propped her up out of the snow.

Now naturally in a hugging position, he felt in his palm something strange, hard and hollow, in addition to the feminine, soft sensation of her body.

At first, he thought she was hiding something in the back of her coat, but he quickly realized that wasn't the case.

Something was inside her.

Mugino's expression hadn't changed. For her, maybe it was natural at this point, nothing worth discussing. Seeing Hamazura's shocked face, she moved her trembling lips and voiced her confusion.

"...What...are you doing...?"

"I'm sick of all this...," spat Hamazura, wringing out his true feelings. "Why do we have to kill each other like this?! Those fights with Item and School were what caused us to be enemies, but wasn't that really a problem the adults in Academy City were supposed to solve?! Their ambition created the darkness in that city, didn't it? Why do we have to go this far just to wipe their asses?!"

"..."

"You, Takitsubo, Kinuhata, even Frenda—you were such good friends before, weren't you?! I don't know much about when you four were still together, but you all trusted one another, even before I was made Item's subordinate, didn't you?! Why? Why did it have to turn out this way?! It wasn't just a short temper that made you kill Frenda. If Academy City's leaders really had control over even that battle, then whatever the specifics were, they set it up so that Item would lose to School, didn't they?! We were cornered, and then they designed it so we'd all kill each other!!"

Academy City's leaders controlled people's fates like gods—had they even predicted this conversation? And were they listening to Hamazura's exhausted words from the comfort of a dark room somewhere, laughing at them?

"Listen. If you want to see me being pathetic, I'll do anything. I'll grovel until I die. I'll lick the bottom of your boots as long as you want, and I'll even light my bankbook on fire. I'd do *anything* if it would stop this fighting."

Expelling his true feelings from the bottom of his heart, Hamazura keenly felt as though his true enemy was coming more and more into view. And it wasn't a monster like Mugino. It was the guys who had turned this lone girl into a monster.

He wasn't going to spout nonsense about it being society's fault, or that their living environment was somehow responsible. A Mugino-level calamity would never happen in a natural environment. She was too massive a nightmare for that.

However.

If there was someone intentionally building everything around the delinquents and espers in those back alleys to create these tragedies and reducing them to means for profit...

Wouldn't *that* be a far more terrifyingly malicious existence than a mere monster?

"So let's...just stop."

They didn't need to fight.

If they took each other's lives, the ones who stood to gain were the bigwigs sharpening their claws in a place they could never reach. Why did others have to wash blood with blood in endless battles just to increase the number of their jewels and paintings? What reason could he possibly have to call this girl a monster—a lonely girl who had been remade into a monster—and hold her at gunpoint?

At last, having ultimately severed the mental chains strung through the giant darkness known as Academy City, Hamazura spoke.

He said what would be the most natural thing for a normal person to say:

"Let's just...stop killing each other."

For a while, Shizuri Mugino was silent.

Embraced by her mortal enemy, so close to her target she'd normally be able to instantly kill him without lifting a finger—the Level Five monster let her body sink into the Level Zero boy's arms.

Eventually, her lips moved.

Her head swung side to side.

"...What are you saying, Hamazura...?"

She seemed to squeeze the words out.

Her voice—it seemed to shatter her own heart to pieces, exposing everything inside it.

"But you chose Takitsubo, didn't you? You killed me twice to save her. And after all that, you're saying you'll save me when I'm like this…?"

"Yeah…," said Hamazura with a groan and a nod. "That's right!! I chose Takitsubo! I swore I'd protect her with my life!! That hasn't changed!! So I can't do it over and choose you or anyone else!! The facts haven't changed at all. I abandoned you so I could protect Takitsubo!!"

He had said he'd willingly endure any humiliation. If that was what it took to stop the fighting. He knew the weight of their violence. When Mugino realized that, the corners of her lips loosened ever so slightly, so subtly that no one who wasn't watching very closely would have noticed.

When she looked back on it, her body had been wrecked.

She hadn't only lost an eye and an arm. Her insides had been messed up badly enough that her missing appendages were the least of her worries due to the effects of Academy City's incomprehensible medical technology and the Crystals ruining her body. As she thought on her miserable state, she said, "…You're so selfish."

"I know. I'm probably the worst person in all of Academy City."

"I killed Frenda, you know. I tore apart Item. And I tried to kill Takitsubo more than once. How exactly are you going to save me?"

"I doubt it'll be easy. And that goes for both of us."

"…?"

"Apologize to Kinuhata like crazy, bow your head to Takitsubo, then cry and beg forgiveness at Frenda's grave. If you do that…"

Then Hamazura stopped talking for a moment.

The Level Zero delinquent used every ounce of his lacking mind to form the words he'd need to get his point across.

"If you do that, we can all be Item again. I'm sure we can!!"

There was no argument.

Far from it—Shizuri Mugino's thoughts had completely frozen over.

In the silence, only Hamazura continued:

"Until then, I'll keep you alive! If you, and Takitsubo, and Kinuhata—all of us—can go back to being Item, I'll stake my life on it!! So stand up, Mugino. Please—just one more time. Stand up on your own two legs, for real!! Break through that twisted pride, the chains that Academy City wrapped around you!!"

"...You, a Level Zero, are going to protect me, a Level Five...?" muttered Mugino before a grin split across her distorted face.

Shizuri Mugino, Saiai Kinuhata, Frenda, and Rikou Takitsubo.

It was the same grin from the days they held strategy meetings together in family restaurants.

"You've gotta be kidding. Don't underestimate me that much."

Brushing Hamazura's hand away, her movements slow, Mugino stood up on the snow. Her body tilted to one side, wavering. He quickly put out a hand to hold her up, after which she used her jaw to gesture to the night sky, with its eerie four-colored trails of light running through it.

An Academy City supersonic bomber was about to pass over.

They could see three lumps falling straight down along the bomber's flight path.

Skreeeee!! An awful scraping noise abruptly ripped through the air. It was coming from the Russian military operative's radio, which had fallen on the snow. The signal was being jammed.

It was probably so that the inhumane acts sure to happen momentarily would never leak to the outside world.

Hamazura felt an intense loathing, like he'd touched incredibly filthy slime.

Hamazura could smell it again—the same smell he noticed while confronting the privateers. This time he was facing weapons from his home, Academy City, but the impression he got from them was the exact opposite of that monster plane that had shot down the Russian saboteur team. These were not the benevolent sort who would blow up Steam Dispensers for them without being asked.

The soldiers on their way now were surely coming to kill them.

That was their only objective.

That was Hamazura's gut feeling.

While looking up at the creepy night sky, Mugino said softly, "...I was apparently disposable to begin with. They probably decided to crush the garbage before she could produce results. Their plan B or whatever is coming down now. What will you do, Hamazura?"

"I already told you."

Hamazura picked up the assault rifle again, which he'd discarded a short distance away.

"I'd risk my life if everyone could go back to being Item again."

"...Hmph. You've got guts," said Mugino to herself so he wouldn't hear.

Meanwhile, Hamazura was observing their surroundings. There would be some time before the Academy City assassins fully alighted. In the meantime, the first thing he'd do was find Takitsubo, who he'd been separated from in the avalanche's aftermath. Once he did that, he had to think of a plan to intercept those Academy City assassins drifting down from the night sky to attack them.

He'd been given precious little time.

A darkness enough to substitute for Shizuri Mugino was about to close in on them to try to swallow them whole.

5

The basement of St. George's Cathedral.

Index's fierce attack was merciless.

She had immediately figured out that Stiyl Magnus was purposely using three flame titans as one to create a combined structure, resulting in less of a burden than normal.

To destroy that structure, she had focused her attacks on just one Innocentius. Under her assault, Innocentius was reduced to two bodies and the unstable stress hit Stiyl all at once.

But the battle continued.

There was no time to rest.

Index's intense attack, which fully utilized 103,000 grimoires, didn't give him that chance.

Foreign things clung to her. In her emotionless eyes shone magic circles; from her limp, unbalanced back grew red wings; and around her floated swords, formed by light particles converging. All of them existed to annihilate any hostile entities, and at the moment, their target was Stiyl Magnus.

"Guh...!!"

Even now, the bloodred wings flapped again and again, and the slender swordlike objects made of light pressed him in an attack that came from multiple directions. The swords were not in Index's hands; they were floating around her. It made Stiyl remember the sword that could fight on its own and kill enemies without anyone to wield it, the one possessed by Freyr, god of fertility.

Angel wings and swords of Freyr...!! Quite the combination, for someone who combines Crossism and Scandinavian myth myself!!

In Scandinavian mythology, there existed no stories of anyone defeating that sword. Even in Ragnarok, the final battle, Freyr only lost because he'd left that sword with someone else before the war began. Nowhere was a method described for what to do to beat the sword.

Yes.

Even Odin and Thor were defeated along with their weapons—but that sword alone was not.

Innocentius wouldn't be enough on its own.

It would be worn down in an instant, then extinguished without time to recover.

Who would stop Index if that happened?

How do I save her? Stiyl wondered.

Roar!!

Without hesitation, he created a flame sword, then stepped between Index and Innocentius.

He had only two flame titans left, so they couldn't buy any recovery time.

Their regeneration couldn't keep up with Index's onslaught, and they'd already lost their momentum as though it had been ripped out of them. If he could make up for that in some other way, he could still fight.

If he could only buy time for them to recover, he'd be able to rotate out.

Zng-bam-zng-bam-bang-bam-boom!! Multiple slashing attacks flew out, blood wings and titan arms swinging. More pressure was building inside Stiyl's body, and an awful sweat dripped off his skin. His flame swords weren't perfect either; he'd been hit by one of Index's earlier attacks, too, which had cut him and violently flung him away. Twisting his body to its limit, Stiyl barely managed to keep fighting.

However.

John's Pen, the Automatic Clerk, was a system designed to annihilate anyone, whether an individual or an organization, attempting to steal the 103,000 grimoires. The fact that Stiyl Magnus was able to deal with her alone at all was certainly unexpected.

Stiyl had grown, but that alone was hardly enough to explain it.

Index was clearly not operating at 100 percent.

The remote-control Soul Arm is hurting her.

Though he was achieving the incredible feat of breaking the 103,000 grimoires' attack on his own, Stiyl didn't overestimate his own ability.

Something extra has intruded on her mind, and it's lowering her precision and speed. If she were in the same state as back then, when I fought alongside that right-hand boy, this sort of parlor trick would never have worked.

Still, he didn't intend to give thanks to anyone.

She wouldn't have had to suffer at all were it not for that thing in the first place.

Stiyl pushed forward.

A momentary opening.

If he detonated his flame sword now, he could knock her out. No matter how great this system was magically, the core was still a delicate girl. If she took the brunt of the shock wave, it should be enough to disable her. And in the meantime, he could put up extra rune cards to bind her mentally.

And then it would be over.

But at the last moment, Stiyl's mind slightly caught on something.

Even if it was to protect her...

Even if the remote-control Soul Arm was forcing her to fight a battle she didn't want...

He'd hurt this child so much already.

Could Stiyl Magnus's magic name tolerate dealing even one more wound to her?

He shouldn't have thought about it. It was time he couldn't afford to spend.

And then—

"Chapter 32, Verse 44. Preparation for counterattacks complete."

—the cold voice of the girl he needed to protect found him.

INTERLUDE SIX

It had been easy to steal one of Academy City's tanks.

For starters, Mikoto was the number one esper when it came to controlling electricity, and while modern tanks still ran mainly on diesel, many of their parts had been digitized. Mikoto could hack directly without needing any cables or dedicated interfaces, so weapon systems like these were no enemy for her.

There were soldiers out there who wore plated armor that would exhaustively reflect any and all electromagnetic waves as defense against electric-type abilities, and some powered suits featured a chemical system to contract springs to avoid electrical vulnerabilities. But apparently those countermeasures hadn't been applied to vehicles.

After stopping one tank's engine from afar and unlocking the hatch, Mikoto had jumped inside and beat up the drivers.

They had tried to raise the alarm, but Mikoto had been interfering with their radio communications, too. Much like how she had been messing with the radars comprehensively monitoring the battlefield and the aerial photography of UAVs. Nobody would notice if she left the battle line.

"Hmm. These go faster than I thought they would," she murmured from within the tank the Sister was operating.

"Modern tanks have always maintained the output necessary

to drive on highways without issue, but going up to one hundred and fifty kilometers per hour on this snowy road must be unique to Academy City technology, reports Misaka offhandedly."

"Well, these hunks of metal cost seven billion yen a pop, so they'd better be able to help at least this much."

"Actually, it's hunks of composite alloys, Big Sister, corrects Misaka. Tanks these days can fire their main cannons at Mach 4.5, adds Misaka idly. That's more output than your Railgun."

"It's not like speed is the *only* thing that matters."

Railgun was just what people called her, and it was the ultimate symbol of electric-type abilities; still, it wasn't as though every bit of her pride was concentrated into only one kind of ability. In fact, her true value was measured in her versatility, her many options to attack enemies from different angles.

…Well, I guess that would put that idiot in a league of his own, since he can erase anything I can possibly throw at him.

"I apologize for interrupting you during your muttering, but—"

"Nyah?!"

"—it seems we've been spotted visually by the independent unit preparing the Nu-AD1967 nuclear warhead, reports Misaka."

Had their full-speed dash worked against them? Their enemies must have seen the snow clouds whipping up in the tank treads' wake through a night-vision scope or something.

Something fired in the distance.

Mikoto's spine tingled—she'd been so worked up over the nuclear warhead that for a moment she feared the worst, but it soon became evident that what just went off was something else. The missiles coming their way were small, but there were a lot of them.

"They appear to be surface-to-surface missiles for bombardment, cautions Misaka. They number thirty to forty."

"Nyeah, yeah."

"It seems you've been acting catlike for some time, but what shall we do? Asks Misaka, urging action."

"Well…" Mikoto hummed as she put her hand on the hatch above her head. She opened the cylindrical, small manhole-sized hatch as wide as it could go, then hoisted her upper body out of the top section of the main gun turret. "I'll do what I do best and fry them up, of course!!"

As she shouted, sparks sprayed from her bangs.

What shot out wasn't a lightning lance. Massive electromagnetic waves were radiating out in a wide cone in front of her, in a way that disrupted the radars used for targeting systems by the surface-to-surface missiles speeding through the air at over twice the speed of sound.

The missiles immediately lost their mark and fell away in other directions.

Several explosions went off, and even though they didn't hit her directly, Mikoto felt like she'd just been slapped across the face. But she ignored it and looked forward.

"Keep going!! If we retreat, we'll just give them time to prepare another volley! We'll take them all out right now!!"

"Mi…Misa…"

"?"

"Misa—serious—kami—electro-interference—sakami—network—sakamisaka—connection severed—misa—emergency—kamisa—restoration—kamisaka-blub-blub."

"Whoa, whoa, whoa!! Are you losing it?! What happened?! Wait, what? You just now realized you have a vulnerability to high-intensity jamming from the strongest ability of your type?"

As the Sister began to writhe into a trance in the driver's seat, Mikoto hastily cut off her electromagnetic wave emissions.

"Phew…A mass-production model could never match the original, says Misaka, reaffirming her own position in a somewhat self-deprecating manner."

Obviously, though, if she stopped the jamming, they'd had no way of avoiding the brunt of the enemy's next bombardment.

"Just charge!!" shouted Mikoto. "If we get close enough, they'll be too afraid of getting caught in the explosions to keep up these huge missile volleys!!"

Vrrooom!! The diesel engine roared as if in response. Not even two kilometers remained between them and the point where the surface-to-surface missiles had originated.

The independent unit seemed to have given up on the artillery attack, but instead, they sent a formation of tanks out from their hiding places behind a hill. Though Mikoto and the Sister's tank could probably survive a few hits, taking concentrated fire from dozens of main guns would undoubtedly be more than enough to turn them into a pile of scrap.

"This is only an estimate, but we'll be blown up twenty times before we cross five hundred meters, says Misa—"

"Then I'll finish things before that happens!!"

A black shadow swayed and squirmed around Mikoto's tank.

No, that wasn't right.

It was actually a huge amount of iron sand, which had been sleeping beneath the snow. Mikoto had ripped every last bit she could find in the surrounding area out to about two hundred meters, and was using magnetic force to have it all accompany her.

From the enemy's point of view, it must have looked like a solid wall.

A wall of hopelessness, like a giant tsunami about to make landfall.

This was what it meant to face the number three Level Five.

Long-range attacks weren't all she had up her sleeves.

Mikoto only knew of two people she couldn't steamroll no matter what, even with this adaptability. Positive and negative. Just two espers, standing at opposite poles.

"Goooooooooooooooooooooooooooooooooooooooooooooooo!!"

Along with her shout, the massive wave of iron sand caught up to Mikoto from above and shot toward the enemy line a step ahead. Like a roaring tsunami, or maybe like a living snake, the mountain of iron sand swept over the enemy's defensive positions at a high speed, and even the Russian independent unit didn't seem able to deal with it.

Of course they couldn't.

A vortex of iron sand wouldn't so much as flinch even if they shot at it, no matter how intense the gunfire.

The tank, driven by the Sister, leisurely plunged toward the center of the chaotic enemy lines. Mikoto leaned completely out of the hatch and focused her gaze straight ahead.

A giant truck-like vehicle sat at the center of the enemy formation. It was unique, with over twenty wheels, bigger even than a passenger car on a train. But the part where the truck's bed should have been had instead been loaded with a very long tube. Stood up on its end using an oil hydraulic cylinder, it was probably the platform for the missile with the Nu-AD1967 on board.

Then, as if to make the situation even more urgent, flames burst from its rear end.

Mikoto took a mighty leap from the top of the tank as it slid sideways over the snow.

...I don't care if it's an ICBM or a strategic warhead with its outer shell replaced. Fundamentally, these systems are controlled electronically. One lightning lance, and it'll be useless.

Using Railgun would be careless—she wanted to prevent any nuclear material from leaking out. Right now, it would be safer and more certain to destroy only the control circuits to turn this weapon into a pile of garbage.

Right as the arms holding the missile in place were about to break away, Mikoto, in midair, focused on her bangs.

With a spark of pale blue, Mikoto yelled at the top of her lungs.

"Blow up!!"

CHAPTER 10

Final Spell Preparations Completed
Rebirth_the...

1

Sasha Kreutzev ran through the Star of Bethlehem.

The Star of Bethlehem: a temple so large you couldn't find anything else like it in Crossist history. Inside, however, it was filled with a terrifying silence. Not a single warrior-monk could be seen: a fact that seemed to implicitly put on display the inner workings of the person known as Fiamma of the Right, this fortress's architect. On a fundamental level, the man didn't place his trust in things like friends or comrades. That was why the fortress had taken this form.

This was where Sasha had been cut off from the young student from Academy City by Fiamma's attack.

Ideally, she was supposed to back him up right at that very moment, but she'd learned in the Elizalina Alliance of Independent Nations that she had no chance of winning in a straight fight. That man named Fiamma was an absolute monster. He'd nearly surpassed the laws of sorcery.

However.

It was a different story if she wasn't up against Fiamma of the Right personally.

...Personal opinion. This temple and the altered night sky are deeply linked to Project Bethlehem's foundation. And chances are high that

Fiamma and the Star of Bethlehem are magically connected so he can control it.

Still carefully observing her surroundings without fail, Sasha darted through the temple's hallways.

...As an addendum, even if I can't challenge Fiamma in a normal fight, it's possible an indirect attack on the Star of Bethlehem will affect him.

In any case, she needed to hurry.

She didn't know the details of that boy's identity, but he didn't seem like he knew any sorcery. The Russian Catholic Church's intrinsic principle was the inspection and removal of the occult, which meant he was someone they needed to protect. The very fact that she was using an amateur as a way to buy time against a monster of that caliber was enough to make her want to punish herself.

...But what am I supposed to target?! The Star of Bethlehem temple is huge—over forty kilometers in radius. Simply searching for an appropriate spot will take considerable time!!

In her haste, Sasha suddenly heard a strange voice from behind the pillars across from her.

"Bum-ba-ba-buummmm!!"

"?!"

Her body stiffened up like a startled cat, and she automatically pulled the L-shaped crowbar off her waist belt. But when she whipped it out for a quickdraw strike, the metal tip didn't pierce the body of the speaker.

What it met instead was the Steel Gloves.

The Soul Arm that looked like a Frankenstein-esque mechanical arm and the crowbar customized for torture clashed, sending brilliant sparks bursting into the air.

The voice belonged to a girl whose outfit resembled a lacrosse uniform with a jacket thrown over it. Most striking was the swaying, manmade, taillike thing coming out of the back of her miniskirt.

"Man, everything was fine right up until I had to use the Steel Gloves to latch on to an outer wall when the Star of Bethlehem started rising up. I tried to construct a line to contact Bayloupe and the others on the ground, but this fortress's defenses were tighter than I thought, and I couldn't open up a hole. Right now, I'm in the middle of memorizing every bit of this fortress's technology that I can—for the sake of Britain's future. I got separated from that crucial boy, and I've been taking little detours to look for anyone who got lost."

Without caring that she'd been hit by the crowbar, the black-haired girl continued. "You're a Russian Catholic, right? You seemed distressed, so I came to give you a rundown of my pricing plans. I suggest the stopover course. And if you act now, I'll throw in a discount."

"...?"

As Sasha tilted her little head, the black-haired girl dexterously moved her "tail" to indicate a direction with its tip. It pointed toward the temple's lower section. She saw several square container-like things hanging there.

"That looks a lot like emergency escape equipment. Kinda like a cross between a bus and a parachute. Well, it looks like Fiamma's plan will work even left alone, and he would probably toss the Russian sorcerers out of the Star of Bethlehem as soon as they presented any obstructions, so I took it upon myself to show them the way before that happened. Heh-heh."

"...Question one. What do you mean by *pricing plans*?"

"Don't get me wrong! I'm not going to take any of your money. My reason for living is to do things that will be to the United Kingdom's benefit. Instead of demanding compensation, I'd like you to promise that you'll help if Britain is ever in trouble in the future."

The black-haired girl spoke with a sly grin.

It made her seem like a devil when paired with the tail reaching out of her miniskirt, but the minor details weren't exactly consistent, making her seem a bit cute. A little devil, so to speak. After all, why was she willing to do people favors based on nothing but a verbal promise?

Nevertheless, Sasha didn't care about what was happening in Britain, so she didn't particularly mention it. "Answer one. Swiftly have anyone escape who wishes to leave the battle front. As an addendum, I don't plan to leave this place yet. I must at least take a parting shot at Fiamma of the Right."

"Eh-heh-heh, roger that. I will come to collect this debt, both publicly and privately, so please do not forget."

With a *ga-gump*, several containers suspended directly below the temple shot off into the night sky. The surface was embroiled in its own conflict, but it wasn't her responsibility to worry about them after that point. They, too, were professional sorcerers, the pride of the Russian Church.

The black-haired girl, waving her tail a little, continued. "Now, what did you mean by taking a parting shot at Fiamma?"

"Answer two. I feel no particular need to answer you."

"You seem irritated. Want some gum?"

Sasha's face, hidden behind her bangs, clouded slightly. "…Answer three. I am unable to understand those who put synthetic substances like that into their mouths."

"I thought Crossist followers have loved sweets ever since the days of manna in the New Testament."

Sasha ignored the girl following her and ran farther through the Star. She hadn't fully grasped this temple's structure, but she had a fairly good guess as to where to find the device she was after.

Something connecting Fiamma of the Right with the temple…

If she assumed that the Star of Bethlehem had a similar layout to a "temple" using Crossist-based modern Western sorcery, then no matter how gargantuan it was, the number, color, position, and other properties of the individual parts composing it should be roughly the same.

Essentially, despite having gathered up the highest-class materials from all over the world and expanding it to maximum scale, Fiamma would still have used the same basic recipe itself. That meant she didn't need to worry about the visual splendor and enormous size. The sorceress Sasha Kreutzev could fight against it just fine using the knowledge she already had.

And then it happened.

Sasha suddenly stopped. But this wasn't the vital temple point in her knowledge; what she was looking at now was a window. Beyond it spread the dark night sky, and she could see another building far in the distance.

Its walls and ceiling had mostly collapsed, and even from here, she could see inside it.

Fiamma of the Right was swinging a sword, long enough that it disappeared beyond the night sky.

And.

She witnessed the moment the right arm of the boy confronting him was severed cleanly from his shoulder.

2

Vasilisa, female leader of the Russian Catholic special forces team Annihilatus, had arrived in Moscow. Several crimson stains marred her already red habit. A liquid of the same color dripped from the edges of her pursed lips, too.

However.

None of it was *her* blood.

With gory hands, crimson even under her fingernails, Vasilisa threw open the front doors of a giant palace. Several killers immediately attacked her, but she didn't pay them any mind: she didn't care about her enemies' combat power nor the fact that they were originally her allies.

She mowed them down...

"Man-eating woman in a one-legged house—"

...in a singsong voice, like a young girl.

In conjunction with Vasilisa's crooning, an old lady wrapped in torn-up shadows went on a rampage through the palace. A huge clump of flames exploded, professional sorcerers were dragged across the floor, and there was a series of screams and angry cries.

When her feet came to a stop deep inside the palace, a large man's voice flew at her from up ahead.

"So you've come."

They were bitter, hateful words.

It was a middle-aged bishop, garbed in gold-decorated clothing. "The *witch* whom the man-eating monster fell in love with. Is that unaging body what you gained at the pinnacle of your destruction of the occult?"

"I'd rather you call me a fairy-tale heroine, Bishop Nikolai. I *am* still a national idol, you know."

"Cease your prattling. You are the remains of a girl who burned her mother and sister alive to obtain happiness."

Vasilisa ignored his words.

She cast her glance forward, and in tandem, the monstrous shadow moved. It shot off in a straight line, plunging straight for Nikolai.

While watching the attacking witch, Nikolai opened his mouth. "The man-eating witch is strong—strong enough to be famous. There are several folktales about her in Russia, but most depict only two options: being eaten alive or being allowed to escape. Almost none of them involves the human killing her."

Bwom!! The man-eating witch exploded.

"However, even the man-eating witch has an exceptional way of being killed."

At the same time, something began to swirl around Nikolai. It was clear water. This was nothing as mundane as regular water, though—when it appeared, the carpet adorning the floor burned to a crisp.

"In one of the stories she appears in, she kept watch over two springs: one filled with the water of life, which could grant eternal life, and one with the water of death, which would end someone's life without question. There were knights who asked the witch to guide them to the water of life, and in the very end, they push the witch into the water of death and take the water of life for themselves."

Engulfed by the clear fluid, the man-eating witch dissipated. Then, Nikolai snapped his fingers. Immediately, a strange water poured toward Vasilisa like a tsunami, threatening to cover her entirely from overhead.

"*This* is the incredibly rare victory against her won by the hands of humankind."

A horrible scene unfolded.

The left half of Vasilisa's body completely disintegrated. Her arm vanished down to the bone. Nothing that could identify her feminine body remained from her chest down to her waist, and the psychedelically colored "contents" seemed almost ready to pour out. And in the meantime, her disintegration continued. Within less than a minute, not even a hair would be left.

"This great war was a national policy signed and executed by the Patriarch himself, the central figure of both this nation called Russia and the Russian Church that controls it," Nikolai said to her, as if spitting the words out. "I don't know what you were thinking, but you should have used your head a little. Then maybe you'd have realized what trying to stop it would mean."

However.

The bishop frowned.

This wasn't right.

Vasilisa's face held no trace of anguish or terror even after half her body had melted. She still wore that impenetrable smile.

And then.

Vasilisa's lips, despite her having lost even her lungs, clearly moved.

"Oh dear. It's quite commonly accepted that coerced signatures are null and void, you know."

Shudder.

The moment Nikolai took a step back, Vasilisa's wounds swelled. *Bk-bk-bk-bk!!* A strange sound rang out, and enough blood and flesh to replace the missing portions of her body began to come together again.

"War-related documents don't go through the Russian Church's command heirarchy, but the military's. And the Patriarch isn't accustomed to relaying orders through a network...He wasn't able to, for example, consider the possibility that after he electronically signed a dummy document with a tablet, that signature data could be placed on something more dangerous.

"Though I don't dislike purehearted, innocent children," added Vasilisa offhandedly.

Despite having been produced in an abnormal way, her newly formed appendages seemed even more youthful and vibrant than before—and brimmed with life. It was the soft skin of a woman in her early teens, looking like it would repel water without doing anything in particular.

Just like a fairy-tale heroine.

"And the only one who could have tricked him was the one appointed as the go-between for the Russian Church and the military—you, Bishop Nikolai Tolstoj. Meaning you were the most suspicious. But what were you after? The Patriarch's throne? If so, were you considering assassinating him amid the confusion?"

"What is happening here?"

Nikolai's eyes tracked over her skin in disbelief, noticing spots that were unnaturally fair and glowing.

"My Water of Death's magic was perfect!! I went through all that to create this Soul Arm from materials I had people search far and wide for, all to deal with your witch!! If you're really Vasilisa, the one under the witch's protection, it should have been impossible to avoid!!"

"My, my. Nikolai, did you forget what you yourself just said?"

Vasilisa, who possessed two different qualities of skin now, as though she had only halfway molted, shook her head with a smile.

"The man-eating witch kept watch over the water of death *and* the water of life."

"No—!"

"Well, yes. The point of the story is the item that grants eternal life—the method of killing the witch was nothing more than a little trick to give the story a happy ending. My flesh is unaging and immortal, and that's no exaggeration—but it's not even worth arguing about which is more important or which is stronger, is it?"

If that was true, then Nikolai had never be able to kill Vasilisa with the cards he had since the very first move. He was fully equipped aside from the Water of Death magic, but even if he used everything at his disposal, he'd be torn apart and her advance would continue.

And Vasilisa was too skilled a sorceress to allow Nikolai to escape.

"Man-eating woman in a one-legged house…"

As the fairy-tale heroine inched forward with a smile, her beautiful singing voice rang out through the palace.

"Please grant your strength to this loyal, powerless daughter. The overwhelming power of a witch, so that I may crush this disloyal, ugly adult into dust and give this tale a happy ending."

3

Round and round.

Touma Kamijou's right arm whirled through the air, blood streaming in its wake. The thin red trail stopped in a ring, creating a bizarre work of art.

Fiamma of the Right casually held out a hand.

Then, as if sucked in, Kamijou's right arm fell into its grasp.

The Imagine Breaker.

The singular right hand, able to erase any and all strange forces, which neither science nor sorcery could explain.

"I have it…"

Fiamma's lips twisted in pleasure.

Pop.

With the sound of a water balloon breaking, the severed right hand exploded into pieces, cleanly dismantling and flaying the blood, flesh, bone, vessels, and nerves inside.

"The Star of Bethlehem has prepared the planetary environment. And I've severed the right hand as well, which must serve as the medium. I can't bring out one hundred percent of the power resting within me without channeling through your right hand, after all. The Imagine Breaker, dispeller of illusions, must have been a sort of purifying function that the sacred right hand naturally possessed, but for me, it's no more than a rat in a pantry, eating away at my reserves. Still, even that unnecessary role is ended now that it has accepted my power as an intrinsic piece...And thus, my right hand is complete.

"Now, if I wield that strength, which should always have been rightfully mine in the first place, to full power, the perfect salvation will be complete. Power enough to save the entire world would have been in my arm to begin with. People may call that *kamijou* or being above God or what have you...but that doesn't matter to me. I've no intent to join His ranks, nor exceed Him. As long as I can gather the power here now and save the world, I will succeed."

Everything was slowly being absorbed by Fiamma of the Right's third arm, which extended from his right shoulder.

There was agony.

Though he never normally lost his cool, his eyebrow very, very slightly twitched in displeasure.

The internalized flesh and blood were perfect, but the Imagine Breaker's power was beginning to whittle away at the source of what made Fiamma of the Right so special.

However, the fact that he didn't immediately lose his strength was noteworthy.

In other words, the power sleeping inside Fiamma was constantly creating such immense power that the Imagine Breaker's effects alone couldn't annihilate it.

...This wasn't something I could do anything about using cheap tricks, but luck and ability seem to have sided with me. Of course, without at least this much output, I couldn't call it power worthy of being wielded by the Son of God.

Whmm. Fiamma of the Right's body wavered.

Not only his heart. His entire body contracted, a pressure building around the third arm. It was probably a reaction to the power within his core drastically moving the third arm, which had acquired true flesh and blood.

As evidence, a huge change occurred, as if to prove the advent of a power that could alter the world.

Not to Fiamma's body.
To the very planet that received him.

The skies opened wide.

Red, blue, yellow, green. Clearly not of this world, the dark of the night sky placed there by man tore open. Giant fissures appeared from many directions, like old stockings ripping, spreading without a sound.

From beyond it appeared a golden light.

It was the definition of myth. A scene out of religious paintings. The sight of the curtain of raining rays seemed to link heaven and earth. If anyone who didn't fully know the circumstances had seen this, they would have instantly thought angels were about to descend from the clouds. In truth, God and angels didn't exist on a physical level, but in an invisible phase, like infrared or ultraviolet rays...but its true quality was, perhaps, similar. After all, that golden light was really a massive amount of telesma.

Fiamma hadn't summoned an angel or anything like that. Perhaps it was more accurate to say he was calling forth the *world* in which angels resided.

Fiamma of the Right hadn't knocked on the proverbial doors of that world many times in bitterness, waiting for the heavy doors to open. No; the very place in which he stood was simply going through a transformation into something that *would* be more suitable for him.

Just as a certain Crossist saint had changed a brothel into a shining preaching pulpit when she was forcibly brought there so she could be harassed.

Just as another holy woman, upon being thrown into a cold, filthy jail, had filled the entire space with shining angelic power, like an immaculate springtime, which had gently healed her wounds.

The heavens are dyed.

The surroundings of the righteous were always dyed in righteousness.

Upon confirming that fact, Fiamma of the Right's lips twisted in pleasure.

Now I need only rearrange the bottom of the earth before the readjustment of all the cogs and the establishment of mechanisms to keep everything in order will be complete, and this world will begin to turn correctly once again, simply as though this is how it has always been.

Which meant he had no more use for the boy who had lost his arm.

He was nothing more than a hunk of flesh serving as an adapter for that right arm to remain in this world, so it would be best to have it make a quick withdrawal.

It will be I, and nobody else, who will save this world. And you are no longer necessary for that.

Fiamma held his third arm, whose physical form was now much clearer than before, out at the boy, who was still spilling large amounts of blood from his horrific wound.

"Consider this an honor, you lump of flesh. I have safely reaped your life's worth."

And that would end things.

This was not the half-finished third arm that had been fluctuating awkwardly.

Nor was this destruction brought on by the amount of knowledge in the 103,000 grimoires.

This—*this* was the power that would save the world.

The power central to one legend.

That which was called *kamijou*. To stand above God.

This explosion of light, massive enough to reduce a planet to dust if necessary, would change the superfluous adapter into so many little pieces without question.

That was the only thing that would make sense.

"...?"

But at that moment—

What Fiamma of the Right felt first was not anger or fear, but doubt.

The boy's body should have been reduced to ashes, but it didn't have a scratch on it.

Far from it.

The immense vortex of light Fiamma had fired had split in twain, scattering to each of the boy's sides. This was despite the beam bearing such gargantuan energy that it could blow away an entire planet and re-create all legends in Crossism.

It was as if...

It was as if an invisible right hand extending from the boy's severed shoulder had repelled it—!!

"What...in the...?" muttered Fiamma, reeling.

The words he murmured weren't enough to keep himself in check—instead, they expanded like a snowball rolling down a hilly road.

"I have absorbed your right hand. So why—*why do you still possess that power*?!"

There was no answer.

The boy, cheeks damp with his own blood, simply kept looking down.

Toward that right arm. Past the wound, at that which should not have existed.

Zk-zk-zk-zk-zk-zk-zk-zk-zk-zk-zzhhhhhhhhhhhhhh-zk-zk-zhhhh!!
An invisible force began to gather.

"..." Fiamma moved only his eyes and looked at what was sprouting from his own right shoulder.

He had certainly taken that boy's right hand. He'd changed it into his own flesh and blood, and within that should have remained the Imagine Breaker, the singular power that could erase all other powers.

Then...what, exactly, was the power gathering within the enemy standing before him now?

There's something...

With a *crackle*, Fiamma felt his lips suddenly drying. He'd finally obtained the Imagine Breaker's right arm. He'd gone through so many grandiose preparations, and after finishing them all, he'd seized that strange right hand—the final key. With Fiamma of the

Right's power and the boy's right arm—which he'd dismantled and reformed as a Soul Arm—he could save the entire world at once. That was how valuable his last acquisition was...

But he'd been eclipsed.

He could barely make it out.

He felt such a threat from the huge tempest of energy concentrating at the boy's sheared-off shoulder that it was causing the color to fade from all Fiamma had gained.

Something transparent...

Fiamma of the Right looked at his opponent's face again.

He couldn't catch a glimpse of it, as the boy was looking down, expression hidden.

Fiamma doubted Imagine Breaker was all that resided in that body of his. But he never thought his mind would be so rattled, so set on edge, just from that ability to cancel out any strange power. Even now, he felt a tingling on his skin so keenly that it almost stung. The impact bellowing deep in his gut, like watching fireworks go off from up close, was almost like a clear wall.

Something is there!!

"........."

The boy—Touma Kamijou—slowly looked up.

It wasn't an exaggerated motion. It wasn't sharp or fast. It wasn't unique, nor was it regular.

He simply looked up.

With just that.

Fiamma of the Right sensed all the muscles from his shoulders to his neck tensing.

It was coming.

He didn't know what, but something was coming—something he needed to be cautious of.

And then.

Booommmmm!!!!!!

Touma Kamijou, with his own strength, gripped that invisible something and crushed it.

*   *   *

Another power appeared above the immense force steadily collecting at the stock-still Kamijou's shoulder, opening up like a giant mouth and engulfing the vast store of power all at once. Almost as though chewing it, the air near his shoulder's gash shimmered like sugar dissolving in water.

That much power.

In an instant.

Into *pieces*.

"...You..."

A murmur.

Kamijou's lips moved.

"I don't know who the hell *you* are."

His words were certainly not loud.

Nevertheless, they stung deep inside Fiamma's ears. His mind was blaring warning signals he couldn't suppress; if he missed a single movement of a fingertip, or the blink of an eyelid, it could utterly change the situation.

"And I don't know what the hell *you're* trying to do."

Fiamma of the Right held the greatest power even in God's Right Seat—and Kamijou *wasn't looking at him*.

He didn't even know *what* Kamijou was speaking to.

"But..."

Maybe only Touma Kamijou knew.

In any case, Kamijou said:

"...you be quiet now. I'll finish things with this guy."

Slp-slp-slp-slp-slp!! A wet sound rang out. By the time he'd heard it, a right arm was already extending from Touma Kamijou's shoulder. Having devoured that enormous power, a piece of fleshy body had been newly produced.

He...abandoned it...? Fiamma tried to mutter, but he realized late that no words were coming out.

The back of his throat dried, leaving only a sticking sensation.

He purposely sacrificed all that power to take back the Imagine Breaker...?

He glanced at the right arm he'd taken from the boy.

Even now, Fiamma had the Imagine Breaker's right hand dismantled and integrated into his own body. But he sensed the light of that power slowly fading from the flesh and blood he'd obtained. The sight made him feel like a concept, a rule, *something* was stating that two powers of this level couldn't exist in the world at the same time. It was as though that "rule" were saying the right arm could only retain its true power when attached to the boy named Touma Kamijou.

Fiamma couldn't afford to lose it.

He wasn't attached to the Imagine Breaker itself. In fact, he'd planned to expel that absorbed function out of his arm at some point. In the process of drawing power into his body, that ability would only be a hindrance. However, if he assumed the "right arm" itself was rapidly weakening, then maybe even its function as a container to hold Fiamma's power would be collapsing. That wouldn't do. Not for his goals.

And then Kamijou said this.

"...I think I'm finally starting to understand."

"Understand what?"

"I'd thought this was a ridiculous plan. This Star of Bethlehem, World War III, the alliance between the Roman and Russian Churches—all of it."

Kamijou paused his breathing for a moment.

The words that came out next were thrust at Fiamma in the form of questions.

"Why did the Star of Bethlehem have to be this gigantic? This is a ritual site so you can safely and accurately do your stupid magic, right? But if Fiamma of the Right was really the strongest being, he wouldn't have had to scrape together all the pieces of churches and temples and whatever throughout the world, would he?"

One by one, Kamijou spoke as though checking items off a list.

"Why did you cause World War III? You said this was to gather the materials you needed from throughout the world and at the same time bring the 'enemy you need to defeat' out into the open. But you can interpret that another way. Fiamma of the Right's power automatically adjusts the strength of his arm based on the strength of the enemy before him. In other words, the stronger the enemy who appears, the more of your power can be drawn out...But why did you want to go that far to force more power out?"

And each and every one of them pruned back Fiamma's layers with precision, steadily revealing what lay within.

"And why did the Roman Orthodox Church and Russian Catholic Church join forces anyway? Why did you want so much power that you'd open the door to other religious organizations, rather than just the Roman Church with its two billion followers? If Fiamma of the Right really was invincible, if he really was someone who could destroy every last enemy, would he have needed to get *underlings*? What I mean is..."

Kamijou spoke.

To continue his words that would be fatal to Fiamma of the Right.

"...you were scared, weren't you?"

Kamijou set his eyes straight on Fiamma as he declared it.

"Because you don't actually *know* whether you have enough power inside you to save the world."

Boom!! An explosion of light flew.

Sharp nails had extended from Fiamma's Third Arm, launching an enormous attack at Kamijou.

But his adversary was not reduced to rubble.

Instead, Touma Kamijou held the tempest of light in check with his right palm stretched before him, then twisted his wrist to force it diagonally behind him.

He was unharmed.

As if to say this was the suitable result for the power that would kill all illusions.

Because of that, his words wouldn't stop.

When he thought about it, this was only natural.

It was extremely, utterly natural that Fiamma of the Right couldn't obtain that sort of conviction.

After all—

"The world hasn't ended or anything," Kamijou continued. "I don't know what it was like a long time ago in the age of legend, but in this era, at least, I've never heard of any world-ending events like the ones in myths."

Words to carve a path to the impenetrable fortress that was Fiamma—words to find a way in.

"And if the world didn't have a crisis that could end it, you'd never be blessed with a chance to show you had enough power to save it. Just like how my Imagine Breaker looks like it has no power unless I'm surrounded by espers and sorcerers."

In other words, the reason Fiamma of the Right had prepared every measure, the reason he had executed such a grandiose plan, was a very, very simple one.

"If you've never saved the world at least once before, how would anyone ever know if you actually had the strength to do it?"

"..."

Fiamma of the Right was silent for a moment.

Eventually, his shoulders trembled.

The man who controlled Red, Right, Flame, and Michael gave a low chuckle.

"...So what?"

The words fell out of him.

Something like a strange, deep-seated grudge leaked from the mouth of the man who had incited worldwide strife and controlled it all completely.

"It's not only me. Nobody living on this planet has *ever* experienced destruction on a legendary scale due to the simple fact that they're still alive. And do you have the right to criticize me for that? Are you saying you've felt power enough to save the world?"

"Of course I have."

But the answer Fiamma received in turn toppled his expectations.

Touma Kamijou even made this assertion without a second's pause, too.

"We humans living on Earth aren't anything special. If you looked down at the planet from a satellite or something, we'd probably all look like insignificant ants. But I've saved them. Call it insignificant or whatever, but I've seen the moment people have saved the world for a single person."

Yes.

Kamijou had been wrapped up in incident after incident in the past. He didn't want to see those he knew spattered with blood in front of him, so he'd always desperately gripped his fist. He was carried off to hospitals all the time, and now even his right arm had been cut off—and his memories? They'd broken off at one point, and beyond that instant, he couldn't remember anything.

So maybe what he'd been able to obtain really was trivial. He did sometimes feel like the result wasn't worth the effort. Simply put, if he'd been stronger, he'd have been smarter about how he went about resolving things. If he'd been wiser, maybe he could have gained much more.

But.

It was for that very reason that he truly felt as though he'd gained something important.

He knew that the things he'd so desperately grasped in his clumsy hands were definitely not worthless.

If Fiamma had been less concerned with the greater machinations of the "world" and simply helped those in front of him, he never would have had to fear how much power was needed to save the world. Even without a grand master plan, or a huge temple, or special traits, or a strange right arm, he wouldn't have questioned it.

But Fiamma hadn't done that.

And that was why he couldn't see it.

Ever.

"Nobody who says they're gonna save the world can protect it."

It was so obvious.

If Kamijou had been acting under the same impression, he'd have lost everything, too.

Under the golden firmament...

To a lonely man who had never gained anything and had never even reached out, Touma Kamijou quietly said:

"Our world isn't so weak it needs someone like *that* to save it."

INTERLUDE SEVEN

Mikoto looked straight ahead.

For some reason, the night sky was glowing with a weird golden light, but she didn't have time to take note of abnormal weather events. A nuclear device was quite possibly about to go off, and if someone *could* be worrying about something like that in such a dire situation, they'd probably get into the book of world records just for that.

"..."

The propulsion flame had vanished from the ballistic missile with the Nu-AD1967 on board. The large missile stood upright, but it was in an unstable position, about to break away from the arms. It didn't seem like it would be able to maintain that position for long—it slowly but surely tilted over. Once it passed a certain point, it fell toward the ground like a tree chopped down by a lumberjack.

Now nobody could launch the missile anymore.

Exhaling lightly, Mikoto glanced around.

Black smoke was rising. It was billowing from the wreckage of the tanks and armored cars the independent unit had been controlling. Everything from their assault rifles to their spare guns had been cleanly cut in two by the friction of iron sand vibrating at high speeds. The carnage was so great that it was a mystery nobody had died.

"...Welp, guess that's it," said Mikoto in a half-hearted tone, searching for the Sister.

The girl she was looking for poked her head out from the hatch of a tank parked in the middle of the enemy formation. "A one-sided display of violence against an entire company two-hundred strong. With what you've done, even I cannot help but feel an inferiority complex building, says Misaka, somewhat glum."

"What're you saying? There are almost ten thousand of you altogether. That's like a brigade or something. And you can use esper abilities and coordinate through the network, and you have Academy City's latest tactics regularly fed into you. You're on a whole other level from these guys."

"I would still appreciate a modicum of individuality," mumbled the Sister before her eyebrow twitched and she put a hand to her headset.

"What? Intercept some Russian military communications again?"

"...It appears as though disorder has erupted—they cannot contact the person named Nikolai Tolstoj, assumed to be the mastermind, reports Misaka with a serious face."

"You always have the same face, though. You mean the enemy's forces are imploding on their own? I wonder if Academy City carried out some kind of raid."

"Details are unknown, but it seems opinion is split between units over whether to continue the operation or not, adds Misaka."

"...There are other units? But if the boss character got done in, that means—"

"It looks like they decided to go on with it, says Misaka, adding the conclusion."

"Oh, come on already! They just had to be super-zealous types!!" cried Mikoto bitterly, venting, sparks flying all about. "So?! Where's the next unit?! Don't tell me they can fire the Nu-AD1967 from a whole bunch of different places at once!!"

"Judging from the contents of their communication, it does not appear to be that bad, says Misaka in denial. The remainder of the independent unit consists of around ten officer-class people who have no direct combat power. And apparently the Nu-AD1967 lying there is the only one they can use, says Misaka, listening to the contents of the communication."

Even if those officers had multiple warheads or missiles, they apparently needed to walk through several processes to fire, like positioning related vehicles and doing electronic adjustments of control bases. And Mikoto had just smashed all the people with the skills necessary to do those things. The remaining officers couldn't set up a new missile, nor could they transport the warhead.

"But they can't fire the missile now that it fell over, right?"

"The officers haven't realized that fact, and they seem to be trying to give the fire order by force from a distance, says Misaka, thoroughly appalled."

Mikoto blinked. "That means..."

"The missile won't launch even with the emergency-use remote command, but wouldn't the warhead still ignite right here? says Misaka, mentioning her own prediction."

"Wait, wait, wait, wait, wait!!"

Misaka, flustered, glanced toward the missile on its side.

"We'd die! If that happened, we'd definitely die!! You said a remote command, right?! Then if I jam it with my ability—!!"

"The signal is optical, using infrared beams, so wouldn't your electromagnetic jamming be ineffective? warns Misaka."

"Gah, come on! What is it, some kind of TV remote control?!"

She doubted radioactivity would leak that easily, but they were still talking about a jack-in-the-box nuclear missile. She walked around it, beginning to observe it. Just the missile itself was over twenty meters long.

"Wouldn't I have shorted its comms circuitry with my lightning bolt from before...?"

"The vital circuits should be secured behind a layer of thick lead and reinforced glass, reports Misaka. And since intercontinental ballistic missiles are designed not to malfunction even when going through cumulonimbus clouds, it should be designed to resist high-tension currents, says Misaka, explaining an obvious thing. Did the missile not stop earlier only because the vehicle-based launch system was blown away?"

"If it's infrared, that means it has a light receiver, right? I should be able to block the communication just by stuffing some rolled-up cloth in it!"

"I wonder if we'll make it, says Misaka, sighing and cheering you on. Do your bessst. Sigh, when will I be able to meet that person?"

"Says the one not doing anything!!"

CHAPTER 11

In Skies Glittering Golden
Star_of_Bethlehem.

1

An intense pressure struck Accelerator's chest.

His breathing stopped.

Obeying some kind of logic beyond his comprehension, the entire night sky tore wide open, and from it, an immense golden light poured forth. Due to the relationship between sunlight and the atmosphere's refractive index, colors that should have been absolutely impossible on the earth blotted out the skies, driving away all darkness from the world. Unlike before, when it was dyed the color of darkness, the dignity of the fortress occupying the skies flew into his field of vision more clearly than before.

Even the night sky prior to now had been abnormal enough, considering the actual time of day.

It had been eerie, as though human hands had pasted it there, and thinking astronomically, the positions of the stars had probably also been utterly impossible.

However.

This gold was in a different class. The only impression it gave was that just talking about it within an astronomical framework was a mistake to begin with, that scientists all over the world would throw in the towel, saying it wasn't possible from a commonsense point of view—and yet it was still there, so they had to give up.

Everything had gone crazy.

The scene, in which science's fundamental rules didn't apply, was of course already mad—but the situation itself, too, where not a single person was trying to *hide* a phenomenon of that scale, spread across the skies all around the world.

In Academy City's darkness, Accelerator had witnessed every incident under the sun and the espers behind them and seen the bleeding-edge technology covering it all up. From his point of view, the scene was absurd.

Maybe in this one second, in this one moment...

Maybe at this very instant, the world itself had undergone a drastic metamorphosis.

But.

...Like I care.

With just a few words, Accelerator ignored the monumental transformation.

His breath was ragged as he brought a slender hand up to grab a spot around his chest.

Last Order's life was still in danger, even now.

In such danger that unless he removed the source as quickly as he could, he would never be able to take it back.

He figured it was selfish.

But even so.

What did he care about something vague like the "world" changing? If there was anyone who declared him a self-centered evil, Academy City's most powerful monster was prepared to take them all on. No matter what he had to fight, no matter how much he had to lose, there was something he needed to do, no matter the cost.

Rescue the girl named Last Order from everything in this unfair world.

Accelerator confirmed his reason for living, here and now.

"Misaka Worst. Did you get the data on the song that got rid of Amata Kihara's virus?"

"Turns out it was pretty easy to find in the Misaka network. It looks like the single, large will in network form sensed something wrong about this song, too. Bet the Sisters were reorganizing their calculation capacity into a parallel system, regularly trying to analyze it over and over. Thanks to that, Misaka got the latest data without having to worm too far in."

After saying the download was complete and putting her index finger to her temple, Misaka Worst gave an evil-looking grin.

Accelerator, without thanking her, said, "The data."

"Just hear Misaka out for a sec. Useless trivia is a reward for head-work, you know. Like a mug of beer after working overtime." She sighed as though disgusted, then took out a portable device from her pure-white combat uniform's pocket. "Misaka got her hands on the song, but her spec isn't right for expressing it. It's not simply a matter of using the throat—judging by the breath usage and the way the sound reverberates inside you, this song isn't normal. In this case, it would be faster to convert it to electrical signals and output it using a speaker. You want the score, the quasi-sound data, or an amplitude graph?"

"Give me all of them. Holding back is for third-rates. Chumps like that would get a pat on the back if they just did it right. Instead, they try to act cool, fuck it up, and then all their achievements are meaningless."

"Gee, *you're* a wonderful person. Misaka would be more comfortable doing it that way, but whatever."

Bzz. A sound like white noise began. Immediately, a change occurred on the device's screen. Several files had been added to it.

Accelerator took the device, then put his fingertips to the screen. Misaka, peering at the small monitor from next to him, said, "But this song isn't gonna be enough, will it? You've gotta replace the exclusive parameters or something. What will you do about that?"

Swinging the device at her to make her move—the back of her head was in the way—Accelerator answered, "I'll manage."

He took something out—a sheaf of parchment.

Written on the sheets, in sticky-looking black ink, were creepy spells and magic circles and what have you from who knew where. The descriptions and contents were indecipherable and utterly disconnected with Last Order, a crystallization of Academy City's cutting-edge technology. Looking at them, even Misaka Worst had to frown.

"...Are you making fun of Misaka?"

"Glad to see you can express so many emotions. Still, guess I wouldn't want the other puppets to learn from you."

"Oh, quit talking like you're our dad or something. That demon-summoning text reeks of the occult. You're telling Misaka the required parameters are hidden inside this thing? Hah! You gonna take a shady twenty-minutes-once-a-day-self-learning course to become an expert spiritualist, then get an angry goat-headed freak to pop out of a pentagram and grant whatever wish you want?"

"No."

"And besides!" interrupted Misaka Worst without listening to him, malice clear in her words. "Last Order's issue has to do with stuff inside Academy City, right? And you think the answer booklet is way out here in some other place? What's that about? Also, you just *happened* to go to Russia, and you just *happened* to run into the appropriate solution? It's basically a video game at this point. They've got hints laid out across the whole path. Now you just need a gun to fight zombies, the hero's sword to defeat the demon king, and a note from a researcher or sage or something, and you'll be fully decked out. You really think the harsh real world is gonna be that convenient for you?"

"...I already said that's not what I'm talking about."

"Yes! Misaka has to wonder about your parenting certification with you pointing a gun at her forehead, no questions asked. I'd appreciate it if you treated her as equal to the other Misakas."

Accelerator had tucked the portable device and sheaf of parchment under the pit of the arm on the crutch and had a lump of metal rattling just under the center of Misaka Worst's forehead as she groaned. But the very fact that she'd bothered him so much and he hadn't pulled the trigger yet would have been impossible the way he'd been before. Academy City's monster really had been through a lot and gotten a little bit softer.

"Advanced security encryption for computers, encryption for drawings during da Vinci's time—both are worlds fundamentally built on numbers. At their roots, they're the same; it's just that they have a slightly different number of digits. Even the encryption guaranteeing privacy on a cell phone can be decrypted by repeating simple calculations over and over. We only think it's *safe* because there are so many digits that it would take too long to decode. It's not like encryption methods themselves are insanely complicated."

"Yeah, and?"

"So I dealt with it using mathematics. I broke all the information down into zeroes and ones and put together the puzzle in my head. Thinking normally, that should have been enough to unravel it. At the very least, I should have gotten a clue to what encryption method was used...Leaving aside how many digits there actually were and how many centuries it would take."

"Should have? Misaka smells the kind of bad luck and frustration she really likes."

"I couldn't solve the puzzle," answered Accelerator plainly. "Numbers by themselves aren't giving me enough pieces to figure it out. I can manage up to a point, but something important is different. Like how if you want to calculate pi, no matter how many times you do it, you'll get a deviation on the hundredth digit. Some other rule set is mixed in with this. If I can't fill in for the missing pieces, I can't fix the deviation. The more calculations I do, the more the deviation gets out of control, until I can't make out anything at all."

"You mean it doesn't matter what the parchment actually says—you can't get the necessary parameters?"

"I can't manage with just mathematics. But I need to do *something* to solve it. So I put every last iota of the knowledge inside me to full use. I may look like this, but I *am* the number one brain in Academy City. Can't brag about it, but I've got all sorts of things stuffed in here. And I did a self-search, from one corner of my mind to the other, pulling out every last bit of knowledge, then more, then more, then more, then *more*."

His words alone continued.

Misaka Worst would have known what he meant. His calculation abilities and language faculties were being supplemented by the excess calculation power of some ten thousand Sisters. Meaning his actual intellectual abilities were absolutely massive.

"And then I realized something."

"What?"

"Something I couldn't understand was already inside me."

"…"

"I realized it during that battle between the angel of water and the angel of science before. But that's not exactly right. I should have physically known it before that—*way* before that."

Accelerator spoke as if remembering something.

"Yeah."

Just talking about his past defeats was something he'd have never done before.

But his priorities were different now.

If he could protect one small life by throwing away a part of his pride, he'd do it without hesitation.

"I couldn't actually *reflect* it. An unknown attack made it right through and cut me in half. I couldn't think of a single way to counter it. I was completely broken back then."

Now, he even had the leeway to give a grin.

He gave himself a push to walk one more step, to walk forward without fail.

"…But that didn't mean the vectors didn't exist. That unknown rule set Aiwass gave me should be inside my body right now."

When he thought about it again, that had to be it.

Aiwass hadn't canceled his ability itself like that Level Zero had.

Aiwass hadn't taken advantage of his ability like Amata Kihara and Teitoku Kakine had.

Aiwass had attacked him directly, sending vectors straight for him, and had crushed Accelerator. That meant its information should have been conveyed to him along with that blow.

The hint had been in his mind all along. The answer had been inside him. Aiwass had told him to go to Russia, but he never said the solution to save Last Order would be left right there in the open. What that monster had offered was no more than the key to the safe.

Don't write it off as unknown.

Don't throw it inside a black box.

You can process the error as is. Set up a fictional vector axis. Think of numbers that don't exist in the real world that are only for solving impractical equations, like imaginary numbers. Reverse-calculate the values from the vectors you see, then bring rules for creating them into focus. Aiwass's existence alone isn't enough to understand. That thing's an irregular monster. Fragments of asteroids transformed by immense heat are nothing more than boulders on their own. But by plugging in advanced numerical formulas, they become the key to inferring the entire expansion of space since the Big Bang.

You might not get a perfect image, of course. But you can put together an extrapolation limitlessly close to the truth.

Even with the Big Bang, said to be the beginning of the universe, the great explosion itself still hasn't been proven. Experts have only re-created and proven several physical phenomena assumed to have happened right after the explosion using giant ring-shaped *accelerators*.

Physicists calculated backward from them, and went through the work of imagining the reality of the primordial explosion as well as they could, filling in the minor details little by little.

He just needed to do the same.

The skill to centrally control energy vectors and convert them into attack power was nothing more than an added benefit. This was where the core of his reason for existence probably slept.

And that ability's name…

At the time it naturally came to him, he'd probably already known, instinctively. Accelerator had only felt that keenly again.

"I can envision the parchment's contents by inputting a single line of a singular physical formula, mixed in with fictional values similar to imaginary numbers. But that stuff's not important. Now that I've solved the puzzle using rules I made for myself, I was able to whittle down the mysterious Aiwass vectors inside my head to a theory extremely close to the real thing, on the same level as the Big Bang theory. Meaning…"

Accelerator paused.

"I've gotten the parameters I need to save the kid. This is where I turn the tables."

He turned to face her.

To the little girl who even now suffered for no good reason.

To the true battlefield on which he needed to fight.

September 30—when he'd confronted Amata Kihara, leader of the Hound Dogs, a doctor named Heaven Canceler had pushed buttons on him that he didn't like. But now, he thought, he could stick out his chest and stand on the same playing field. He understood the value of fighting to protect a single life, the nobleness of struggling to keep her flame alive.

Brawls weren't the only kind of battles.

Victories didn't only mean taking from others.

Before now, he'd vowed to reign as the paragon of villainy to protect those important to him from the unjust darkness. In bloodstained back alleys, he'd massacred one shithead after another—trash like himself—and lost many things in exchange for winning those death matches, continuing to be swallowed into even deeper darkness.

But this battle was different.

As he was now, he no longer needed to be a villain…!!

"…Hmph."

Accelerator looked down and mulled over that thought for a moment.

He thought it over very deeply.

When his face came up again, his eyes held none of the hesitation from when he'd been wandering Russia.

"I'm starting."

He kept it short.

He didn't need any particularly flashy action.

He just had to close his eyes and give voice to the "answer" in his mind.

Then it would end.

It would all end.

Brwwaaaahhh!! Enormous numerical formulas began to flow into the world in the form of song.

Was Misaka Worst, watching beside him, surprised? This wasn't anything special. Accelerator already had experience removing a virus with his own strength—the one from Ao Amai. The system was just different, that was all. Which meant he should be able to do this. He had everything he needed. If he maintained himself in the best condition possible until the end, and produced results like a machine would, that would be enough.

That should have been enough.

But he felt a slight tug in the mechanisms that were supposed to be running smoothly.

An ominous micro-vibration, like one portending a train's complete derailment.

The golden sky...?!

The pressure weighing down from directly overhead possessed the same sort of mysterious vectors as Aiwass. Yes—with this, he figured, it wasn't strange there had been slight interference with him and Last Order. Anyone standing close to power lines with high-tension currents in them would be able to hear white noise like on a television or radio. It was the same thing. Having figured it out instantly, Accelerator worked slight corrections into his calculations.

He imagined a ball rolling down a hilly road.

Down the hill was a cliff.

If he continued to correct his calculations like this, he'd cross some sort of ultimate line. No matter what he'd deciphered, Accelerator was currently a being who lived in the normal, physical world. He only happened to know about this mysterious rule set. He wasn't steeped in it himself.

He'd have to cross that line.

He'd be swallowed up by that mysterious rule set.

He knew it—but he didn't stop. He plunged forward. He shot straight down the hilly road. The cliff was already in sight. Accelerator took the deep hole beyond as a gate. He faced forward, without hesitation, flying into that bottomless darkness.

He passed through it within an instant.

And then, immediately after, something went wrong.

"...???!!!"

Crkkk. Something inside him screamed. The blood vessels on the back of his hand swelled abnormally. He keenly felt the thick pipes of blood running from his fingertips to his shoulders. Right after realizing that, the rupture occurred. His skin broke from the inside, and a dark-red fluid rushed out all at once.

Had he realized it?

The voice was too unique, using breathing impossible for normal humans, wildly flailing around the vibrations of sound not only in his throat but through his whole body, then producing it from his mouth—he was refining mana from his life force, building a spell, and outputting it onto this real, actual world...Did he realize he was performing true, genuine sorcery?

Espers couldn't use magic. If they tried to anyway, what waited for them was an intense physical rejection.

The damage didn't stop in that one spot. The flow of his arteries and veins and nerves strung out through him like a spiderweb rose to the surface of his mind with eerie throbbing and anguish. They were making their locations plainly known due to the compression his internal organs felt. A huge amount of sweat burst out all over him, more than if he'd suddenly entered a sauna. That clear, disgusting liquid mixed with something else, something red. Accelerator felt like little parts of his body were exploding.

And that sensation wasn't inaccurate.

But he still continued.

Because he couldn't stop now.

"Oooooooooooooooooooooooohhhhhhhhhhhhhhhhhwww waaaaaaaaaaaaaaaaaaaaaaaaahhhhhhhhhhhhhhhhhhhhhhhhh!!!!!!"

A gruff but sublime voice, similar to primordial dancing songs of indigenous peoples, spread through the white lands. Even with every part of his body soaked in blood and countless wounds pushing apart from within, those notes never broke for a moment. It was the strength of his will that kept him going—he wanted to save this one little girl, and those feelings alone overcame the real-world pain, allowing him to do advanced mental operations without even tiny errors.

There was a story like this, once.

In the days when Crossists were still persecuted by the Romans, many disciples going through horrific torture had, apparently, sometimes seen the shadows of angels.

The more boring types believed these were illusions caused by an oversecretion of brain matter to escape the worst, most terrible pain. After all, an angel appearing would be far too convenient. If a creature called an angel really existed, if such a grand being would side with them, then they would have massacred the Romans on the spot to begin with.

And maybe part of that was right.

But what if the disciples, who had passed into the extremities of the mind, had unconsciously gone through the mental labor to elaborately conduct huge and complex spells, temporarily controlling telesma to perform advanced acts of summoning? Couldn't one have an opposing viewpoint, one a little more fantastical? Couldn't one interpret it as actual angels coming for them, if only for a moment, in response to their mental voices and through the momentary spells they wove?

Yes:

Accelerator was praying.

With all his heart. Without asking for anything else. Without even paying attention to his own pain. Academy City's strongest monster kept on praying—to save something more precious to him than his own life.

When that white angel, who had fallen to the depths of the earth through immense malice, had tried to crawl back up in search of light, its wings had been broken by another monster.

But could anyone think he was still forsaken after looking at his blood-covered face?

Wouldn't they have to think that, even if he had fallen to the bottom of hell, his radiance had never clouded?

For example:

The many devout who had been physically abused, thrown into jails or brothels, and yet turned those horrifying places into shining places of faith.

The soul was not sullied merely by where it stood.

When sinners confronted their sins and risked their lives to make up for it, it washed away that black darkness.

It wasn't just any performance.

Nobody was forcing him to do this.

This world was not so cold that it would refuse to grant salvation to those who truly and sincerely repented for their sins, kept on the struggle to change their hearts, and tried to break the shackles of their fate. Among the historically important figures in Crossism were some who were originally Roman and caused Crossist disciples to suffer. But they regretted their actions for their entire lives, and when they continued fighting to make up for their unatonable sins if only by a little, they forged a path to salvation alongside their suffering.

Who was Accelerator right now?

Was he a good or a bad person?

A human or a monster?

Science or sorcery?

If one had asked him, he'd probably have said this without hesitation.

It's obvious: The only word for who I am is me.

"Gaaaaaaaaaaaaaaaaaaaaaaaaaaaaaaaaaaaaaaaaaaaaaaaaaaaaaaaaa aaaaaaaaaaaaaaaaaaaaaaaaaaaaaaaaaaaaaahhhhhhhhhhhhhhhhhhh hhhhhhhhhhhhhhhhhhhhhhhhhh!!!!!!"

At the end of the bloodstained path he walked, Accelerator severed every chain he'd bound himself with.

Nothing remained to fetter him.

He could go as far as he wanted.

He would forge down this path he believed in, to save that small life called Last Order.

Bloodying himself to do it.

Continuing the song.

And...

2

Where had Rikou Takitsubo gone?

With his battle against Mugino over, plus confirmation of additional attackers' descent from a bomber, what Shiage Hamazura needed to do was meet up with Takitsubo as fast as possible. Even if they put together a plan, he didn't want to stay separated.

"Damn it!! Where are you?! Takitsubo! Where are you?!"

As he shouted her name, Hamazura was grabbing a thick branch. He was digging on and on, scraping away at all the snow at the foot of the mountain the avalanche had caused. He'd been separated from her around when his fight with Mugino had started. If he wasn't getting any answer even after searching every nook and cranny of his surroundings and shouting in a loud voice, it was possible she was actually buried under snow.

Even in extremely cold regions, when doing manual labor, it was natural to sweat and get thirsty. Hamazura took a gulp of some carbonated water from an aluminum can. It remained water because he'd had it inside his parka the whole time. If he'd left it out, it would have quickly frozen.

Meanwhile, from a short distance away, Shizuri Mugino watched Hamazura in his confusion, seemingly bored.

"Hey!! Help me look for her, Mugino!! I can't find her anywhere! I don't have any clue where she could be!! Help me out here! I need as many hands as I can get!!"

"Why should I?"

"Crap, what now? Takitsubo is still far from fit even with the Crystals' strain reduced and leaving her out in the cold like this would be unthinkable and I have to warm her up soon because she's weak she's a weak girl she's a girl in a lot of trouble because of those Crystals!"

"..."

Academy City's fourth-strongest Level Five, Shizuri Mugino, Meltdown, lost it.

With a *boom*, a lump of snow right next to Hamazura vaporized along a straight line. The intense force caused a water vapor explosion to go off, sending Hamazura's body into the air.

"Whoa—crap. My head is spinning. It might be the Crystals... the *Crystals*, do you hear me...? ...affecting me. I think there are a bunch of other ways to propel a body—but no, I might just take the most beautiful fall you've ever seen."

"What did you do that for, Muginooooooooo!! Who knows where the frail little bunny-type Takitsubo could be buried, come onnnnn!!"

Face-first on the ground, Hamazura's voice as he shouted was a girlish falsetto.

"...You're such a damn pain. I just helped you dig."

"Noooo!! Please draw a line between gags and serious stuff next time!! This is awful—I knew it! A completely harmless healing-type character is all I need!!"

Mugino gave him an incredibly unenthusiastic look and pointed behind him. "You mean the one sneaking up on you right now?"

"Uwaahh?!" screamed Hamazura, without meaning to, at the ghostly girl, Rikou Takitsubo, who had quietly approached him.

In any case, now they were all together.

With Mugino and Takitsubo, he confirmed the situation.

Then he looked up at the golden skies.

Amid the psychedelic scenery, he could see a dropped Academy City assailant about to land on the ground a short distance away. They wore a black combat uniform that didn't match the white snowfield—the kind of thing that might be supplied to urban special forces. He couldn't spot any sort of firearm.

"..."

She seemed to have fired it by momentum before, but Shizuri Mugino's Meltdown would be useless in battle at this point.

She might be able to "fire" a few shots, but that would be as much as her Crystal-ravaged body could take. And firing at stationary targets was one thing—he didn't know if she could hit a real enemy moving quickly and irregularly. However he looked at it, it wouldn't be possible to wipe out the enemies about to approach with nothing but an attack that had such a harsh usage limit.

Rikou Takitsubo wouldn't be able to provide any combat power in the first place. They'd been able to relieve the adverse effects of the Crystals to a certain degree but not so much that it fundamentally cured her. Besides, even if she was at full strength, she was meant more for rear support. She couldn't use her ability for battle, and she certainly didn't give the impression of being especially skilled in limb-based melee combat.

The attackers would know that.

That was why they'd made such an obvious approach by dropping out of the bomber. Otherwise, they would have been a little more careful.

Hamazura jumped into the conifer forest. A few dozen meters ahead...

He held his breath and watched the shadows as they moved without haste over the snow, slowly but surely getting closer.

They weren't normal soldiers.

Only the gold and white of the flat masks covering their faces departed from their fully black uniforms; the masks were strange, looking over twice as wide as their faces. They didn't feature any holes for the eyes or mouth. The entirety of their masks glistened with artificial light, like LED decorations for a cell phone, evidently able to depict patterns using several colors of light. Sometimes they would produce faint, indecipherable lights; Hamazura didn't know what they meant. Judging from their constitution and the parts of their head and jawbones not covered up by their mask, the attacker was probably male.

"…"

The situation wouldn't get any better if the enemy himself was the only thing Hamazura looked at.

He checked the surrounding area, searching for usable weapons.

Since Mugino and Takitsubo wouldn't be any help, fighting together wasn't a good idea. He had the girls evacuate to a cave near the woods. Hamazura had to fight the attacker while drawing the attention of the rest away from the cave.

Gripping his assault weapon in both hands, he flicked the bulky safety with his thumb.

…Did they want light, nimble movement in exchange for armor?

Hamazura stared between the trees at the unknown masked assailant from dozens of meters away.

With how thin his gear was, it seemed unlikely there would be a ballistic plate in it, but given the situation they'd brought this stuff out in…Maybe it was better to assume some good-for-nothing effects had been added with good-for-nothing tech.

Special fibers might hold the bullet back, but would the impact still get through? If it can, then 7.62mm bullets will get him. I think Anti-Skill's armor is thicker, at least. He can probably move pretty fast in it, but maybe I can manage if I get him before he notices me.

Then it happened.

Whoom! The assailant's neck turned his way.

He wasn't holding anything that seemed like a firearm, but if he had electronically contracting springs reinforcing him—like Hard Taping—then he could rip a person in two with just his bare hands.

There was no delay. Hamazura's hands bounced up, aimed the gun at the assailant, and pulled the trigger.

He felt an impact like he'd been punched in the right shoulder.

His first shot had hit a tree trunk on the way. His second headed straight for the attacker.

A shrill noise rang out as sparks flew.

The rifle bullet didn't pierce his target, however. Wings, which had an extremely biological appearance, had suddenly extended out from the middle of his flat gold-and-white mask, unfurling like a shield and covering his slim frame.

"Wha—?!"

Hamazura thought he'd stop breathing, but not simply at how those organic wings had appeared.

Letters had appeared—letters he knew—lighting up the mask covering the attacker's face.

"Equ. Dark Matter."

Wasn't that the nickname of the second-strongest Level Five in Academy City—the one Shizuri Mugino had faced?

He heard a *clack.*

The assailant was getting ready to charge toward him.

"Oooooooooooooooooooooooooooooooooooooooooooooohhhhhhh hhhhhhhhhhhhhhhhhhhhhhhhhhhhhhhhhhhhhhhhhhhhhhhhh!!"

Screaming, Hamazura kept firing bullets on full automatic.

Ping-ping-ping-ping-ping-ding-ding-ding-ding-ding!! Sounds of little pieces of metal getting shaved away rang out in succession. The spat-out cartridges ran into one another in midair, adding noises to the gunfire that were similar to bells ringing.

However, they were not the sounds of the attacker's body being pulverized.

They were the sounds of every single rifle bullet bouncing off the multiple white wings that had poured out of his big, flat mask.

They wouldn't reach.

As despair began to swirl in Hamazura's breast, the assailant moved.

Roar!!

Flapping all his wings, he closed a dozen meters in a mere instant.

There was no room to dodge.

He continued, ramming into Hamazura like a cannonball.

A dull creaking noise burst out from inside Hamazura's upper body.

"Gahhhh?!"

Maybe it was a good thing that he could even scream.

His body flew several meters through the air before falling onto the snow. He felt hard roots pushing up against his back. With that attack alone, the taste of blood spread through his mouth.

Swoosh. The sound of something cutting through wind rang in Hamazura's ears.

Multiple wings extended from the assailant's gold-and-white mask, undulating like whips, lashing out into the entire surrounding area.

Hamazura rolled on the ground, stifling the scream clinging inside his throat.

Several of the conifers comprising the forest were torn through like paper. The ground nearby was gouged out, and a thick tree began to fall with a *craaaaack* toward Hamazura as he continued to roll.

The white wings and mask were made of the same stuff.

They spread out unnaturally, like heat extending sculptured candy.

"No…," muttered Hamazura.

He'd never actually seen Teitoku Kakine use his ability. But something fundamental was wrong about this that let him understand it anyway.

"That's not Dark Matter—that's not even an Academy City ability…?"

The assailant didn't respond.

Instead, he slowly brought his white wings to bear on Hamazura.

"?!"

Hamazura frantically got up and tried to retreat to gain distance, but then a different impact hit him from directly behind. This set of assailants wasn't alone. Hamazura had only just now realized that, but it was too late. The trunk of the conifer behind him was torn through in one swipe as multiple white wings attacked from right behind him.

It was probably fortunate that the cut-down tree trunk hit him instead of the white wings.

However, the hammer-like impact still slammed into him.

This time, he couldn't even scream.

After falling onto the white snow, he noticed the red stains around him. He'd been hurt so badly it had taken him a few moments to realize his own body was bleeding.

Lying there, he looked around to check his surroundings.

Three of them, and those were only the visible ones.

He had no idea when or where the last one had been hiding.

"Esper abilities are like flames."

One of the attackers spoke.

Because he was wearing the same mask, Hamazura couldn't tell which of them was opening his mouth.

"Flames are a powerful weapon only humans can control, to be sure. But simply flailing flames around makes it no more than a primitive man's torch. The civilized use flames to strike metal—and so it is with abilities."

I see, thought Hamazura.

Level Five abilities, like Shizuri Mugino's Meltdown and Teitoku Kakine's Dark Matter, produced effects that didn't obey the regular laws of nature. So what about the new matter produced using that power? Didn't it create an entirely new structure of matter, one which entirely ignored the derivation of elementary particles, atoms, and molecules that had been going on since the Big Bang?

Just like how carbon nanotubes were different from simple lumps of carbon. Just like how semiconductors using advanced calculations were different than lumps of glass. Just like how steel processed at high heats was different than soft metal.

A new substance created using energy not of this world would have properties not of this world.

Enough to disparage a true Level Five ability as a primitive man's torch.

"...Don't get too comfortable," spat Hamazura. "Did you give the Crystals to Mugino so you could use the flame called the fourth strongest as a weapon, making her into some kind of flamethrower stuffed with naphtha? And it didn't work out, so you came to grab her before the embers went out. Now what will you do? Hook her up to medical equipment and change her into a blast furnace for manufacturing a new form of matter?"

If that was the case, the project would have no need for Hamazura.

He was already on the run from Academy City. They'd kill a Level Zero without a doubt.

The masked assailants closed in on him from three directions.

He couldn't beat them with just one assault rifle. Plus, the Level Five they were based on was strong enough to tackle entire army units by himself. Whether he brought out tanks or hand grenades, he'd never be able to take down even one of them.

That was right.

So if he wanted to fight them head-on...

Shiage Hamazura hadn't stood up against them just to stay quiet and be killed.

"Hey," he said, still on the ground, relaxing his arms and legs. "I was rolling around like that for so long that my pocket spilled out somewhere. Know where it went?"

The assailants ignored him.

They'd swiftly kill the two rebels, recover Shizuri Mugino, and return home.

That was the only thing on their minds—but then, suddenly, they felt a hard, gravelly sensation at their feet.

It had sharp, clear shards. Like the remains of a broken glass container.

"Damn it. That was my only hope," he murmured as though he'd given up on something. "...I finally picked up the item I needed to negotiate with Academy City—and now you're ruining it!"

A bad premonition swelled within them.

Still lying on the ground, Hamazura said this next to the assailants who were supposedly in a position of absolute superiority:

"That package was the bacterial wall the Russian saboteurs were trying to spread around. You didn't have to go and crush it right in front of me like that."

The air around them immediately froze. The assailants, too, being part of Academy City's underworld, had heard about the bacterial wall used in the Kremlin Report and how it worked.

It was an airborne pathogen, and the mortality rate of those infected was over 80 percent. It was extremely resistant to high heat as well, so simply boiling it would be ineffective. Because of that, sterilization required the usage of toxic, high-density ozone. Also worthy of note was that the effects of the germ were strong enough to decompose oil, meaning there was a risk it would eat through the filters and such on existing biochemical weapon masks, vehicles, and buildings. When preserving it, most of its activity was apparently contained by keeping it in a super-low-moisture container, but once it left the package and came into contact with the moisture in the air, it wouldn't be possible to keep it in check any longer.

Yes.

Even with special masks and suits covering their whole bodies, they could still be infected!

"Shit!!"

For the first time, the assailants panicked. Even realizing it would do them no good, they began to move, trying to get as far away from the broken glass container as possible.

And then it happened.

Shiage Hamazura quickly waved the hands grabbing the assault rifle.

"I lied, morons. It's a can of fizzy water."

"?!"

By the time his attackers figured it out, it was too late.

From his prone state, Hamazura got up onto his knee on the snow and forced his body forward. He shoved the rifle's barrel in between the white wings, forcing open a line of fire toward a spot near the attacker's waist.

He didn't have time to hesitate.

He pulled the trigger.

After a sharp crack of gunfire, one attacker fell down into the snow like a door being violently kicked in. He'd been protected by the white wings before. It was plain as day what would have happened had the bullets hit the attacker anywhere else.

"You bastard!!"

They'd probably never even considered one of their own might die. The other two attackers flapped their wings hurriedly.

At that rate, Hamazura's body would have been torn to shreds. Not even the thick conifer trunks would obstruct their pearlescent wings.

However, a dead human body outfitted with the same technology now rested at Hamazura's feet. He turned around, then dove behind the white wings that were still extending from the grounded corpse. Their wings, which would shear through anything, were blocked by wings of the same material and bounced away.

Hamazura kicked the dead body, drastically changing the angle of its neck—or more specifically, of the wings coming out of the mask. In the direction the head was facing, the white wings rushed down at the attackers from directly overhead like a guillotine.

Their weapons were the same, so of course, his foes could block the white wings swinging at them, too.

One attacker produced several wings from his mask, using everything he had to stop the onslaught. Yes—everything he had. His dire straits left him no room for anything else. And then, Hamazura thrust his assault rifle's muzzle toward him from the side.

A scream rang out.

With a short burst of fire, red fluid sprayed, and the second assailant fell to the snow.

But that was as far as he could go.

The third assailant went on the counterattack. Several white wings writhed, not going for Hamazura but instead gouging out a huge chunk of the ground at his feet. If Hamazura lost his balance, he wouldn't be able to aim his assault rifle; he'd be completely disabled. After securing his own safety first, the assailant unwaveringly went forward. He grabbed Hamazura's neck in one hand. Then, with one side of his body positioned in front, he slammed him into the trunk of one of the conifers still barely standing from the battle.

"Gah?!"

The impact shot through him, his breathing stopped, and his assault rifle slid from his grip. Hamazura's feet were floating off the ground. The assailant, saying nothing, spread the white wings from his mask wide. Not a shred of mercy could be felt from them.

"…Aren't you forgetting something important?"

But Hamazura grinned.

He grinned, and he spoke.

"No matter how unstable her physical balance got because of the Crystals, Shizuri Mugino is still number four. She can manage to fire a few times."

"…" The assailant, still holding Hamazura up by one hand, shook his masked face slightly. "You're bluffing. You can't trick me like that twice. Shizuri Mugino's power was clear the moment she lost to scum like you."

"I see. That's too bad."

Hamazura relaxed his hands.

With his limbs hanging down, he said one last thing.

"At least you'll die proud of yourself, then."

An enormous ray of light burst forth.

By the time the assailant had perceived it, it was already over.

His right side was forward, and his right arm, which was grabbing Hamazura's neck, was blown off at the shoulder. That's what it seemed like, at least—but that wasn't actually what happened. His right chest had been completely torn off along with the right arm. Everything up to right under his neck had transformed into a cavern.

With a thump, Hamazura's body fell to the ground. The severed arm was still digging into his neck.

"Wha...what...?"

In shock, the attacker looked back along to where the light ray's firing source was and, a few hundred meters away, saw two girls standing there. One looked exhausted, wearing a yellow coat, and the other one was in a pink tracksuit. The one in the tracksuit had her shoulder under the yellow-coated girl's arm to hold her up.

Shizuri Mugino's balance was unstable because of the Crystals, and she was not in any state to fire precisely. Even if she'd had the strength in reserve to fire a few shots, she wouldn't have been able to hit, so there shouldn't have been an issue.

Which was why...

Rikou...Takitsubo...You're telling me number four borrowed someone else's help to correct her aim...?

The assailant didn't realize his own words were no longer coming out of his mouth.

No, that's not all. Even that bacterial wall bluff...It was only an opening move. If we'd had the information that Shizuri Mugino would be coming after us, it would have been easy to deal with them... He made us think it was a crazy possibility, just a bluff...and that put us off our guard, giving them the opportunity to take careful aim so they could hit for sure...

A few shots would have been able to wipe out the assailants.

If they all hit exactly where they needed to...

If they'd dodged even one, it would've been over. Actually, if they used the white wings coming out of their masks, they would've been able to repel it, seeing as it was only Meltdown.

So he...

Hamazura had taken the assailant down with the assault rifle out of nothing more than pure luck, beyond their plan. His job was to slow them down, buy time, and let Mugino's power finish them off.

The wounded number four couldn't have fought alone.

So they'd altered the playing field so that she *could*, even injured.

The assailants had fallen for every last one of their schemes.

"Damn it…all…"

The assailant's deeply gouged body swayed unsteadily before sinking into the snow.

But his mask still moved.

With the power he had left, he tried to take Hamazura with him.

Until the assailant felt something hard on the side of his mask—on the side of his head.

It was the muzzle of an assault rifle.

"I can't…believe it…"

The man belatedly regretted his mistakes.

Their orders had stated their first goal was to kill the Academy City rebels Shiage Hamazura and Rikou Takitsubo. Underestimating their opponent as a Level Zero meant they had failed to properly analyze their true combat strength.

"So this is…Shiage Hamazura…"

"No, it's not."

The young man pointing his assault rifle muzzle downward as he wobbled cut him off with a few words.

Then he said:

"This is Item. And don't forget it, even if you end up in hell."

3

There hadn't been any reason.

His right arm just had a special power.

For example, assume a nuclear missile was about to be fired right in front of you. Say in your hand you held the control key, and the console that controlled its launch was in front of you.

In that situation, would it be strange to insert the key and stop the launch? Wouldn't it actually be stranger to say something like *I'm not an expert, so I don't understand* or *It's not my responsibility to risk my life when I'm not a soldier or police officer* and just stand there idly without doing anything?

Someone like that wouldn't be human.

They'd just be a toy with its power switched off.

He hadn't needed a reason to fight. In fact, he'd felt guilt at doing nothing with the great crisis unfolding right in front of him. And he'd gathered the necessary quantity of the required components. From the start, he'd never tried to reach out for something he couldn't attain—instead, he'd prepared over a long period of time, slowly, like arranging wooden boxes to form a set of stairs.

All for a single success.

For a victory that needed no greater reason.

And *he* had to be the same, he thought. Their natures were different, but they both had right arms possessing singular capabilities. And in actuality, he'd used that right arm to continue fighting. He'd probably never doubted the reason in the process. After all, he didn't need to think about it. He had no reason to stand still, in fact.

And so they'd be fighting in the same way.

They should have been.

They should have been, but...

Ka-kreeeeeeeee!! A high-pitched whine echoed over the Star of Bethlehem.

It was the sound of Touma Kamijou's right arm deflecting the flow of Fiamma of the Right's third arm.

Kamijou's Imagine Breaker couldn't cancel enormous power sources involved all at once. But he'd taken advantage of that condition. When an attack from Fiamma came, he'd position his palm on the side of it, pushing it as if to move a train onto another rail; sliding it away to divert the enormous attack's trajectory.

How? Fiamma demanded.

His right arm's output level varied depending on the strength of the enemy he had to defeat. And right now, Fiamma had designated his target as the calamity called World War III, which could destroy the entire planet and pollute the surrounding space with huge amounts of debris. The Star of Bethlehem, Misha Kreutzev, the flesh and blood of the right arm serving as the Imagine Breaker's vessel... If he was successfully drawing out the appropriate capacity—then the current Fiamma should have had the power to emerge victorious alone over science, sorcery, and the war itself in which all that was mixed.

It was equivalent to the power to send all humans on Earth to the grave. He was trying to use it for salvation, but depending on its application, he could probably wipe out all of human history in an instant.

And yet...

"...How are you able to stop it?" he murmured.

He reaffirmed his grip on the remote-control Soul Arm.

In the skies, golden lights converged, and as Fiamma's third arm moved, so, too, did those lights rain down upon Touma Kamijou.

"It has that much ability? All it can do is erase preternatural powers!! All it *does* is grab whatever force it can't fully cancel out and bend it!! ...My right arm can sink an entire continent into the ocean in one swing. It could dry up the oceans with a single thrust!! You were an adapter, and all you were supposed to do is hold on to that flesh and blood until the promised hour. The stem of a potato, returning to the earth once the harvest is over—and nothing more!!"

Guided by the 103,000 volumes, the power of salvation bared its fangs.

A rain of gold began to fall.

It showered down on almost half the Star of Bethlehem's surface. Clusters of stone buildings toppled, one by one, and huge cracks appeared in the floor on which Kamijou and Fiamma stood. The pressure shoved the explosion out in every direction, and its destruction was so massive even Fiamma unintentionally covered his face with his third arm.

However.

Touma Kamijou did not fall.

His right hand was aimed straight up. He'd forcibly repelled the initial attack, then caused it to burst like a milk crown. He'd caused its aftermath to strike the deluge that followed, twisting the light rays' paths completely.

How?

That boy's right arm couldn't have had that much power in it.

In the first place, no human could ever land even a single attack on Fiamma in his current state. It could be Vento of the Front or Acqua of the Back—though he could end them with a single swing of his right arm.

"You still don't get it?"

Touma Kamijou's mouth opened amid the ruins, the bombing from the skies having blasted away the ceiling.

His voice was low and heavy.

"You told me, remember? Your right arm's power varies based on your enemy's strength. The stronger your opponent, the more power you can draw out. And to get the maximum power out of your arm, you caused World War III to amplify the darkness in people's hearts. In order to bring the enemy you needed to defeat out into the open and finish setting up for all this."

So what?

Even now, as they spoke, World War III raged on. Tragedies were begetting tragedies, and the maelstrom of malice was spreading to every corner of this planet. Fiamma had multiplied his holy power by responding to that ugliness, and once his preparations were complete, he'd purify the entire world.

"But in that case, you could also say this."

Kamijou rotated his right arm as if to feel out his shoulder, and as his joints cracked, he continued:

"What if everyone's hearts aren't as filled with malice as you think they are? Then you wouldn't be able to draw out the power you envisioned."

*   *   *

Fiamma's eyebrow twitched.

He glanced beyond the shattered walls, down toward the surface far below. Though the golden skies illuminated it, he couldn't see past it. Maybe dust and vapor particles were overlapping in the air, forming a screen. The sight looked like the smoke shooting from the minds of those causing wars and killing one another, covering the world.

"...That's a bold assumption."

Fiamma of the Right shook his third arm.

He gripped the remote-control Soul Arm tightly to receive the support of that boundless knowledge.

Clear hatred shone in his eyes.

"This world is twisted. Control will never appear again. Even the basic four aspects ruptured beyond repair without me to fix them. Remaining resources, clashes between tribes, differences between religions, food shortages, state warfare, the destruction of the environment—all of it is tangled together so badly it's now impossible to resolve them one at a time, in order."

"..."

"And you would so boldly claim that I couldn't reap the amount of malice I expected? You must be joking. That's the sort of rubbish someone who didn't know the meaning of the word *malice* would say!! The war is still going on, you know. And this great conflict is making everyone act to their hearts' content!! Nations, tribes, religions, genders, languages, capital, bloodlines, talent—every single one of those little thorns pricking everyone's minds has begun to spill into the outside world!! ...You want to believe that people's hearts are really that pure deep down? Humans would most certainly do all these things—what part of their hearts are you even looking at?!"

"You're right. I can't see people's hearts from the outside. Maybe a human's essence really is something dark and grimy. Maybe I just don't realize it, and even I have malice inside me I'd never want to believe was real.

"But," noted Kamijou.

He would not end there.

"A human's true nature is greater than that."

"What…?"

"How can you say for sure people only have one side to them? If we have black malice deep in our hearts, then who are you to say we don't have another side to us besides that?"

That's right, thought Kamijou. A person's heart was host to an incorrigible expanse of darkness. Humans were creatures who thought about more than just connecting with others. They also had qualities that led them to avoid others for many reasons: to protect themselves, to ensure their safety, to possess something. They were made so they could naturally take action that would hurt or eliminate others.

But light slept in that space, too—an equal amount or perhaps more. The kind of goodwill you'd normally be too embarrassed about to mention out loud. The level of justice that didn't even feel the need to make itself known. Those sorts of things surely existed. You just couldn't see them—but they were absolutely there.

It wouldn't make sense otherwise.

If human hearts really only held malicious intent for killing and taking from others, civilization would have died out by its own hand long ago. The fact that they'd survived this long, the fact that history continued without interruption, clearly proved that the will to connect was stronger than the will to destroy.

"I didn't need a reason."

Touma Kamijou made a fist with his right hand again.

"It's not because I was strong—you failed on your own. People don't need a reason to be able to fight for those they hold dear. They don't need special powers to be able to fight for what they want to protect. That's the power that saved *me*."

"For no reason?" Fiamma watched Kamijou as if looking at something unbelievable. "That conclusion only applies to *us*. For example, assume a nuclear missile is about to launch. We have the control key, and the console is right in front of us. Sure, we don't need a reason to put the key in and stop the missile from launching. But people that don't *have* the key can't do anything to stop it."

"Nobody needs a key." The argument didn't even take a second to come out. "You could just stick a wire into the keyhole. Or you could pop open the console's lid and plug a laptop cable in, too. And you could probably shoot a cannonball at the missile just before it launches. There's always more than one way to solve something. It doesn't give you a reason to stand idly by and wait silently as the missile launches...Everyone has the right to fight—fight for something you'd die to protect, even if you have to take on the entire world."

That's absurd, muttered Fiamma. For the first time, he'd been forced to realize that this creature called Touma Kamijou was fundamentally different from what he'd expected.

"You're gonna give Index back."

A declaration.

Touma Kamijou took a big step forward.

"And not just that. The UK and Academy City—and the Roman and the Russian Churches. All that quibbling, all the fighting between science and magic, all the countries crushing one another in World War III—I'm ending all of it right now."

"You think you can?"

As if to counter Kamijou's approach, Fiamma of the Right spread his third arm wide.

His lethal arm whose destructive force increased depending on people's hostility.

"Do you think you can win this enormous war without losing a single thing?! This pathetic world war is nothing but *prep work*. And the purification of the surface has already begun in response to the Star of Bethlehem. You *still* think you can score a free victory?!"

"Sure I do."

On one side, the shadow leader of the largest denomination of Crossism, thoroughly bolstered by the aerial temple, the Star of Bethlehem; the worldwide malice, brought into focus through World War III; the knowledge from the 103,000 grimoires; the natural gifts of God's Right

Seat; and the flesh and blood of that singular right arm he'd severed and stolen.

On the other, a high school student who had a unique right hand but otherwise no special traits.

Yet, there was no need to be afraid.

And so, Kamijou advanced ever forward.

"Unlike you, I believe in how strong humans are."

Meanwhile, a deformed shadow appeared off the coastline of Barcelona, crashing against it.

An aberrant, golden form, about one hundred meters long, like a giant arm or an enormous snake. A hand, reaching toward the sky—its five fingers half opened, standing tall, grasping nothing.

The populace watched in trepidation. After all, this area was relatively far from the flames of the great war; the region wasn't even in a state of alert.

As all the civilians looked on, the golden arm changed.

Brk-brk-brk-brk-brk-brk-brk!!!!!!

From the ground to its fingertips, the golden arm began to swell explosively from within. Within moments, the palm's form broke down, changing shape like a huge balloon.

The distorted sphere made a *creeeak-greeeak* noise as it reached its limit.

And then...

Simultaneously, a massive hand burst out of the Sea of Japan. It clenched tightly, as if to crush itself.

What emerged a moment later was a rupture. A massive shock wave spread out in every direction, crushing even the gargantuan hundred-meter arm itself to pieces.

Boom!! It was as though a huge space station had crashed into the water's surface. A radial wall of seawater over thirty meters tall spread out in all directions.

Carriers, escorts, amphibious assault ships, battleships, cruisers…
It engulfed Academy City and Russian forces alike as their myriad
ships of metal stood lined up in battle formation.

"What's going on…?"

Seeing the massive catastrophe closing in on them, a navigation
officer belonging to an Academy City affiliate let out a groan.

In this situation, he couldn't even decide: Was it better to seek shelter inside the ship or put on a life preserver and jump into the sea?

"This isn't even a war anymore! What the hell is going on with the
world?!"

At the same time, a similar golden arm had exploded on the eastern
European front as well.

What happened there, however, was not a high wave.

Radiating out from the ruptured arm was a thundercloud at zero
meters above sea level. The deep-black mass of water vapor licked
explosively over the surface, and at the same time, the entire space
rang out in a freakish sound. Sparks. Over a billion volts…The extreme
high-pressure current would cause those swallowed in the thundercloud to burst into many pieces, and it would fry all the electronic
devices loaded on board with their weapons.

"No way…," muttered an Academy City man to himself, bewil-
dered at the approaching dark cloud.

The scale of this calamity was just too big. The thunderhead
spread out to the sides, extending several kilometers; at this point, he
couldn't avoid it no matter where he ran. And if it engulfed him, his
body would explode in a matter of seconds.

The man donned a thin smile at the insane situation—but then,
somebody grabbed his ankle. It was from the underside of a wrecked
Russian armored car. He lost his balance and got pulled inside.

A moment later, the black cloud rushed over him from forward to
back.

Crackle-crackle-crackle!! There was a series of eerie noises, like
train tracks shorting out. Even under the vehicle, he wouldn't

emerge unscathed. Part of the electric current, traveling through the ground and climbing up to him, zapped through his entire body without mercy.

But he didn't die.

As the Academy City man moaned, it finally dawned on him.

"You...," he murmured, seeing the female Russian soldier who had pulled him in. "Do you understand this? We're *enemies*. From your point of view, I'm an evil invader."

"An invader who would go to such lengths to stop the Kremlin Report? Anyway, this isn't the time to be squabbling over the war anymore. Our chain of command is in shambles. We're getting unconfirmed reports of things like this happening all over the world."

Glaring at the snow, blown up from the ground and still tingling with purple lightning aftereffects, the woman spoke as though spitting the words out.

"I'm fighting to protect my family, too. Like hell I'll sit by after coming this far just because we're facing down the apocalypse or the extinction of humanity or whatever this is!!"

Crack-crackle-crack-crack. They heard a sound like water suddenly freezing over.

Immediately after, there was a massive *wha-bam!!*

Some sort of huge ring had appeared on the surface of the ground visible from underneath the armored car. A material like pure gold with a radius of over a hundred meters—the giant ring was wider than a four-lane highway, and it was stuck into the ground at an angle.

It's almost like an angel's halo, thought the Russian.

More than that had changed, however. As if to follow along with where the thundercloud had just licked the surface, a bundle of riblike parts connected to the huge ring drew arcs through the air as if they were sharpened tips. Following that, bundles of cloth traveled in curved, riverlike lines, appearing one after the other and gouging out the ground and blowing away nearby parts of the conifer forest. Pushing themselves into this world by force, it looked like a giant toy box being overturned.

It was a flood of enormous structures spreading out in all directions. Each and every one was a ridiculous size.

Attempting to speak despite his throat suddenly drying out, the Academy Man whispered hoarsely, "...What the hell is going on?"

"Damned if I know," answered the Russian soldier as if to push him away. "The only good thing about this is that we're on a snowfield. If this thing happened in a city area, it would topple all the buildings around it."

"Also..."

A huge roaring vibration tore through the air.

The black cloud had withdrawn, but the dangers hadn't ended.

There was no rule saying there could only be one golden arm.

As long as those giant arms kept bursting out of the ground like this, there was no telling what dangers awaited them next.

"Another one. What now?!" demanded the man.

The female soldier ran a finger over the antitank rocket launcher. "Should be obvious. Finish things before it ruptures!! Give me a hand, Mr. Academy City. I need your city's firepower!!"

"Shit. I had my hands full stopping the Kremlin Report, you know!!"

"Your end goal's the same. Doesn't matter if it's a bacterial wall or some occult bullshit—we just have to wipe off the face of the earth every last thing that'll needlessly kill people!!"

Meanwhile, in the Strait of Dover, a golden arm about to rupture was cut through diagonally from the middle, then began to sink into the sea.

Civilian and soldier alike were utterly dumbstruck.

Amid it all, only the girl who had put a final end to the golden arm moved, twirling her staff.

The girl was around twelve.

"Hey, Mark!! You slacked on the symbolic weapon prep, didn't you? I'm not even getting eighty percent output from this thing!!"

"Boss, isn't the symbolic weapon's user supposed to be the one to produce and consecrate it?"

"Pff. Anyway. Never thought I, of all people, would be pitching in to help the world out."

"Judging by the situation, Fiamma of the Right is trying to purge the surface by spreading purifying telesma and altering everything starting with fundamental structures. He seems to want to save the world."

Mark continued, wondering aloud if everything on top of those structures would change, too, if their foundations changed. "...But that's a lot of it. This much telesma all over the place is going to have destructive results. And unlike the mana refined in human bodies, telesma contains elements from the start. We're seeing an outbreak of each aspect—or of things derived from them."

"Basically, it's the great flood Noah built the ark for. For shameful humans, this overblown sense of cleanliness *is* a catastrophe."

The blond-haired girl referred to as Boss gave a wicked grin that didn't match her age.

And yet, it held so much force it made it seem like no expression was more suitable for her pretty features.

"And we call shameful humans *shameful* because they're really bad losers."

Boom!! She heard a distant explosion.

It came from the horizon. Even she wouldn't be able to eliminate all the golden arms. An empty ocean surface, with no people or boats, was low on the priority list, so "explosions" like that had been happening sporadically.

Moments later, things like giant angel halos and bones began to appear inside the calamity's affected area.

"...I see. He didn't forget the aftercare, either. He's collecting the resources he'll use for the 'restoration' after washing the world clean—how nice of him. That's a lot of stuff, and it's all more valuable than pure gold, or platinum, or tungsten. And more convenient."

"Well, telesma makes up everything from an angel's body to its clothing and weapons, so I suppose it's possible to convert into matter…but for someone using *human sorcery*, I can't help but be baffled at the sheer scale of it."

"But it won't matter," said the blond girl quietly. "True—if every person on earth had enough resources to be satisfied, it might solve most of the wars in the world. Individuals would settle things on an individual level. But that won't work. If you give people resources, they'll use them to expand their control. Someone could use a rocket to go and take over the moon's surface, and you couldn't stop them. Then they'd use the moon's heavy hydrogen to aim for Mars next. Having a larger amount of resources won't stop wars. It'll only make them bigger."

"On top of that, human technology can't manufacture materials equal to angelic arms and armor. You wouldn't hurt them with lasers or diamonds, and I doubt human sorcery can do anything to an angel's body. Those things aren't resources—if anything, it's just bulk-sized refuse."

"Well, our goal is to command the entire world, sorcery and science alike. No point controlling a world if it's going to be washed away, leaving us with nothing but piles of logs we can't use. I guess we'll have to work hard for the cause of good this time."

Wha-bam!! Several more golden arms burst out of the ground and the sea.

The girl didn't pay attention to them.

Putting the staff she'd been twirling onto her shoulder, she unflinchingly took a step forward. Then, using a megaphone handed to her by a man in full uniform, she shouted to every corner of the battlefield.

"Listen up! I don't care if you're with the UK, or France, or Academy City, or Russia!! Any unit that can still move needs to support us with equipment that can transmit infrared-targeting information! As soon as we receive the coordinates of a target, we'll come and provide full support for an attack!! From now on, it's time for some bombing—of the people, by the people, and for the people!! Let's raise hell, baby!!"

The petrified British soldiers, who couldn't put together the words they needed to say, opened their mouths anyway.

"Wha…what…? What is…? Who *are* you people…?"

The girl didn't turn around to answer.

With many soldiers trailing in her wake, she put her mouth to the megaphone and lobbed over her shoulder as though singing, "A sorcerer's society. The Dawn-Colored Sunlight."

Elsewhere, Acqua of the Back, standing in a white snowfield, spotted a deformed silhouette breaking through the snow on the ground to show itself.

Academy City, the Russian forces, science, sorcery—none of it mattered anymore. Everybody charged the golden arm as one.

They wielded their weapons to crush the source of the calamity before an even greater rupture could occur.

All to defend those precious to them.

...How foolish you are, Fiamma.

Acqua smiled faintly.

This man who almost never changed his expression had smiled—only a little, but it was unmistakable.

It will not be you nor I who saves this world. No matter what you destroy, no matter what you bless, the people will no longer submit. I suppose it was obvious that those living in this world would defend it.

In that case, the time had come for him, too, to wield his power as one of those people.

Acqua was no longer a saint. Nor part of God's Right Seat. He didn't have the strength to lift the Ascalon, his greatest weapon, and the amount of mana he could refine had fallen to a level comparable to a regular sorcerer.

But what did it matter?

Acqua didn't fight because he was a saint or because he was part of God's Right Seat. He didn't think he'd led a praiseworthy life by any means. But unfortunately, he was attached to this world—because he could envision someone he wanted to protect.

Meanwhile—

"There you are. Finally found you!"

An old man muttered quietly to himself, moving his face away from the binoculars.

The young man next to him sighed in his direction. "Is it all right? Russia was probably the worst place to come back to. I've even heard rumors that the old name of your group, the Astrologers' Brigade, is still stuck on their blacklist."

"Would you shut up? It's about time I used those Soul Arms I've been stockpiling for myself, isn't it? Besides, when you got the information William Orwell was headed for Russia, you were the one who tried to go after him without even reporting it."

"I'll admit I let the blood go to my head. I still have a debt to repay from the Knights of Orleans business. If I let that go, it would leave a bad taste in my mouth." The young man who answered him held a French sword called a colichemarde, derived from sporting equipment. And next to him stood a woman able to use a spell called the Revelations of Arc.

They weren't the only ones. Many had gathered here; that was how many people the mercenary had saved on the path he'd walked.

"How is our mercenary doing?"

"Same old mercenary. But something's not right. I feel like it would take more than that to get him in a playful mood."

"Are you worried about him?"

"Of course not."

The old man sighed haphazardly, shaking the Japanese katana resting on his shoulder.

A Thundercleaver.

A modern, mass-production-type Soul Arm based on folklore wherein a group of swords had intercepted strikes from the very heavens themselves.

And as if in response, hundreds of figures behind the old man readied their own preferred weapons.

"If he has that much charm, it'll be worth fighting alongside him."

"But…," said the young man. "We're just treating the symptoms. Those calamities are springing up all over the world—I don't think it'll put an end to them."

"I know that. That's why we're the former Astrologers' Brigade. People who have crossed all over the world have a huge network to match. In fact, it means we can freely work in lines we'd never be able to connect with just the stubborn ones who'd set up shop in one place to defend it."

"?"

"Well, connecting those teeny-tiny threads is about all this old man can do. Someone more suitable will take care of the real hard stuff...After all, at their roots, they're no idiots, either."

After saying what he wanted to say, the old man shook his Thundercleaver.

"We're free spirits, and what we need to do is simple. Do you know what that is, youngster?"

"Not to think about anything complicated," said the young man, smiling and waving his colichemarde in the same way, "and to take up our swords when someone needs protecting."

All they needed were the two words *Let's go.*

As one, they pushed toward the battlefield.

At the same time, a woman named Vasilisa, head of the Russian Church's special forces team Annihilatus, kicked a sorcerer who was once her subordinate and sent him flying, slamming him into the locked double doors like a cannonball and destroying them.

She was in a palace in Moscow.

There was a massive *ga-bam!!* It made the person confined in the room jump out of his skin.

This person was a boy about fifteen years old. He was slender and had a more curvaceous beauty than even Vasilisa, an already beautiful woman, and he was so thin he'd probably go to his eternal rest in three days if abandoned out in the wild. Even his majestic attire, created for the Patriarch, fit him even worse than a little kid wearing his father's suit for fun, dragging it around behind him.

Spitting the blood in her mouth onto a random spot on the carpet, Vasilisa gave a sweet smile. "Why, hello there, revered leader of the Russian Catholic Church. What a luxurious birdcage they've thrown you into—it looks like they took good care of you. Fairy tales would normally have reversed the positions of the young man and heroine, but in any case, I'm here to rescue you from the evil demon lord's castle now!"

"...To think anyone would still call me the Patriarch. I never had any real power. No matter how much I shouted, nobody would even leave me a weapon. Everyone held up my forged signature as an indulgence and didn't listen to me when I asked them to withdraw."

"I'll forgive you, since you're cute," interrupted Vasilisa in an obviously jocular tone. "And there's still something you can do. Something only the Patriarch can do."

"?"

The Patriarch tilted his little head so adorably that even Vasilisa, who only ever thought about Sasha Kreutzev, nearly felt her mind swaying. The method she used to decide what side to take was very simple. While unconsciously putting a hand to her face to make sure she didn't have a nosebleed, she thought, *Jeez, would you stop that? I've already lost more blood than I can probably afford...*

"Can you see that?" Quelling her impulse to agonize over his cuteness, she pointed out the window.

Even from here, they could physically see the fortress floating in the golden skies. It had just that much scale and altitude. It was the temple of Fiamma of the Right, of God's Right Seat, which had come to be called the Star of Bethlehem from remaining fragmented sources.

"That fortress was formed from the necessary parts in the necessary quantities from Crossist churches and cathedrals throughout the world. But each of those buildings has its own form. You can't fuse them all just by collecting them in one place."

"What are you...getting at?"

"There's a spell to connect them." Vasilisa waggled her finger. "Fiamma used the Roman Church and the Russian Church. He used both kinds of spells to their maximum effect to give that fortress its structure."

"Which means…"

"If you analyze it, you can break the fortress's joints. I'm sure Nikolai Tolstoj was the one who provided the Russian Catholic spell, but there was no evidence of it in his palace. Still, though, that doesn't mean we have to give up. Understand what I'm saying now?"

Naturally, the spell being used was probably a secret among secrets of the Russian Church. It was unthinkable that Fiamma would use something so easily analyzed as the keystone to his final plan.

However…

"I get it." The Patriarch moved a slender finger and rubbed his cheek. "There's a facility nearby for reproducing and managing scaled-down versions of phenomena, right? It runs all sorts of experiments by making one-to-one-hundred-scale building dioramas to figure out what conditions cause ghosts and spirits to appear…"

"If we remove its limiter, it can be used for Russian Catholic magic, too—the kind people use. And if the simulation goes well, we could go backward and figure out which spell Fiamma used."

"And you want me to remove it."

"Mm-hmm! Think you can? I do have the man-eating woman in a one-legged house, but that doesn't mean I can guarantee your safety."

The Patriarch, on the verge of having his head patted, deftly moved his head to escape Vasilisa's hand and headed for the room's exit. Not realizing how his behavior had actually caused her to shudder, the Russian Church's leader asked, "The Star of Bethlehem's joints use a Roman Orthodox spell in addition to our Russian Catholic one, don't they? We might not be able to weaken it all by ourselves."

"…Things will be fine on that end. I got a stubborn old man to help me—a weird one, who had a weird number of contacts—and had him connect the teeny-tiny threads."

"Ah?"

Accompanied by the shade of an old, wrinkly woman as she followed the Patriarch, Vasilisa gave him a simple answer.

"What I mean is that it turns out those people aren't as rotten as everyone thought."

*   *   *

Meanwhile, Matthew Reese, the old man who had abandoned his position as the pope of Rome, had delved far below the great Vatican cathedral. His goal was to analyze the spell Fiamma had been using for his plans. The spells a single member of God's Right Seat could use probably couldn't have completely covered the utter scale of his project. Leaving what was central to it aside, it was highly likely he'd used an existing Roman Orthodox spell to fill in the gaps.

"Hiya, you dandy gentleman. How's it going over there, hmm?"

"Hmph. Should I be the one you're calling? I'm no longer the pope."

"I thought I was speaking to the leader of the Roman Orthodox Church in both name and function. And besides, Peter Iogdis wouldn't have been suitable for our adorable Patriarch."

"By the sound of it, you got your audience with the Patriarch. I've finished sorting out the important documents myself. I'm now constructing an ultra-long-distance spell circle that can interfere with the Star of Bethlehem currently hanging over Russia."

"Oh, how convenient. I see the Vatican has all sorts of secret tricks up its sleeves after all. If my subordinates could get that kind of funding, we could do whatever we wanted, too."

"Anyway, how reliable is the theory that robbing the Star of Bethlehem of its power will cause the disasters on the surface to stop as well? I'm getting reports of golden arms causing mayhem from all over as we speak."

"Hmm? It should be fine, shouldn't it? The surface disasters are happening in response to the celestial ones, after all. I'm almost certain if we stop the celestial disasters, all the others will go away, too."

"Fine, then. Even if we stop Fiamma, it wouldn't mean anything if we forced sacrifices onto everyone else."

"By the way, I take it this is all okay for the Roman Church?"

"What are you talking about?"

"Fiamma of the Right isn't compatible with us. But the fact is he's been giving incredible benefits to the Roman Orthodox Church until

now. If you shatter that foundation yourselves, doesn't that mean the Roman Church may not reach the same kind of prosperity as before?"

"It doesn't matter…A power that cannot protect is meaningless. To save the people, I will hold Fiamma in check, even if it means reducing the Roman Orthodox Church's power."

"It sure is a crime to be so adorable."

"…What? Now what are you talking about?"

"Oh, just our leader over here. And how maybe you had a time when you were like this, Gramps."

"My nature did lead others to look up to me, but it never cast me in a such a light. I was chosen to be the pope, after all. They probably thought I was a stern father symbol or something."

"Oooh, that comment is making our adorable father symbol get all angry. But he's so cute!! And I'm going to hug him!!"

"…And that light is one mainly cast on fairy-tale *heroines*, is it not?"

Rather annoyed, Matthew Reese scanned the innumerable documents sleeping in the basement. There was a huge collection of books in this library, where a little girl named Index had once been invited.

If he could learn what spell Fiamma was using, he might be able to use it to mount a counterattack. He might even be able to stop this great war.

But that would mean…

"We're contributing to our own defeat, aren't we?" uttered the young priest who had followed after Matthew Reese.

"This isn't a defeat," corrected Matthew, voice firm enough to sever the hesitation of others. "We are fighting for victory. Even now."

"That victory won't gain us anything."

"If you truly thought so, then you wouldn't be taking the same action as me."

The young priest fell silent for a time.

Only the sound of pages turning continued.

"…Will we be able to start over?"

"Yes," said Matthew. The old man even smiled. "We certainly will."

That was when it happened.

Matthew scowled slightly. A moment later, a stabbing headache dug from his temple all the way across his skull. The knowledge in this treasure trove was so pure they had to invite the Index of Prohibited Books here. Even the man who was once the pope would experience severe physical and mental effects from prolonged viewings.

"I can still keep going," said Matthew Reese as the young priest hastily put out a hand to try to give him care. "I can still fight. To open a path to a hopeful tomorrow, we can't afford to stop now."

In truth, however, he had concerns.

Roman Orthodox secret ceremonies and Russian Catholic wisdom.

If they took advantage of their technical information used in the Star of Bethlehem, they'd be able to deal significant damage to it.

There was no clear guarantee, however, that they'd be able to tear it from the sky.

After all:

Those aren't the only techniques being used.

He'd received a report that Fiamma of the Right had stolen the remote-control Soul Arm for the Index of Prohibited Books. Which meant the techniques being used weren't only Roman Orthodox and Russian Catholic.

Yes.

The final key was…

"The English Puritan Church's archbishop…"

"Hey, I have an idea. Want to play rock-paper-scissors to decide who gets to talk to that vixen?"

Simultaneously, in the Star of Bethlehem floating in the Russian skies, Sasha Kreutzev pulled an assortment of tools out of her belt. She began to draw a huge magic circle, using her L-shaped crowbar to make marks in the floor.

The one losing her head was Lesser, who had been preparing a container to escape in.

Several metal container-like objects equipped with giant parachutes hung from the bottom of the fortress. Lesser had been going to each in turn, getting them ready to use.

Apart from the two girls, over two hundred Russian Catholic sorcerers, used and discarded by Fiamma, were present here, too. They had to let them all flee to the surface in stages before Fiamma disposed of them.

And also.

Even if it started to look like they *could* defeat Fiamma, it wouldn't make a difference if they couldn't find a way for everyone, including Lesser and Sasha, to escape.

They were still at an altitude of ten thousand meters.

"Wait! I don't know what you're trying to do, but the last flight is taking off soon!!"

"Answer one: I'm not here because I want to be. As an addendum, my feelings are that if we are going to leave soon, I want to do it right now." Sasha didn't stop working her tools as she answered. "As for my opinion—despite saying that, I do feel resistance to fleeing without doing anything. In reality, the only one fighting Fiamma is that boy. As a professional sorcerer, I must support him, even in vain."

"But how?!"

"Answer two: Fiamma used my body to summon the POWER OF GOD and change the heaven's condition according to his wishes... Which means I myself might be able to become a factor that drives a wedge into his plans."

She didn't know how far-reaching the effects would be.

At the very least, Sasha Kreutzev's actions alone would never prove a setback to Fiamma's grandiose plans.

But she'd do it anyway.

The light in Sasha's eyes, hidden by her bangs, never wavered in unease.

Lesser, for her part, scratched her hair half-heartedly. "Grr!! Then I'll make you finish quickly!!"

"?"

"It's true—I'd like to stick here until the very last moment if possible. That boy seems like he'll be a boon to the United Kingdom, after all. I'll help you out so I can kill time before the limit."

"Answer three: You don't need to go that fa—"

"Either way, it seems that when you chose that route, it forced our escape plans to take a time-out."

Lesser used her thumb to point behind her.

Some Russian Catholic sorcerers had climbed out of their escape containers and were walking toward them.

To spread even more intricately the magic circle Sasha was trying to draw.

With Sasha surprised, Lesser grinned and said, "We're not stopping this now—not until we get results. We might as well get in our parting shot at Fiamma's plans while we can."

Elsewhere, a band of girls wearing mainly black nun's habits were racing across a Russian snowfield.

Their clothing seemed Roman Orthodox, but their current location meant they were far, far from home.

It was the former Agnes unit.

The two-hundred-odd Sisters were heading for a place where Academy City and Russian soldiers had fallen.

Battles could be decided on a lot more than killing enemies.

They had their own fight to win.

"Sister Agnes, rescue targets spotted. It's impossible to evacuate them all outside the explosion's effective range. As planned, please use the rescue target distribution map to calculate points for shelter construction!!"

"Listen well, Sister Angeline. The shelter applies the theory of Jesus's swaddling clothes and manger! All nuns specializing in the usage of Mary-type ex-votos are to give instructions immediately upon constructing each shelter!!"

"The large rescue helicopters are standing by three thousand meters behind us! Please get the heavily wounded on board before the next explosion occurs!!"

"The lightly wounded should head to the shelters! We don't have enough time to get everyone onto the helicopters!!"

It happened in the blink of an eye.

The things they were calling shelters were nothing more than tentlike structures made of wooden frames and big white cloths. However, they shouldn't have been able to erect them in a few seconds to half a minute. To an unknowing observer, they may have looked like automatically expanding spring-loaded toys.

They began to carry fallen soldiers who could no longer move to the shelters set up in the middle of the battlefield, one after the next.

Both the Academy City and Russian forces were baffled.

They were all humans, and all had the same reaction.

If they'd realized that sooner, maybe the war wouldn't have gotten so out of control.

"...What...are you do...?" croaked out a man who had been operating an Academy City powered suit. He'd asked the question even as various parts of his body were being wrapped in bandages. "Who are you...with...? Whose side are you on...?"

"Oh, but we did not come all this way to discuss things such as those," answered one of the black-clothed nuns. "But if I was to answer, I would say our only goal is to reduce the damages of this war by as many individuals as possible."

"..."

The soldiers were speechless as they watched the Sisters, who were using medicine made from plants rather than the antibiotics they were so used to. To fill in the science, a communication came in to the wood-and-cloth shelter.

A man's voice echoed from what looked like a card taped to a shelter column. *"Sheesh. Fiamma sure is a neat freak. We had no idea his big cleaning spree would be this widespread, man."*

"Then this is part of Fiamma's purification operation after all?"

"Probably best to assume so. Not only is he destroying the pre-established harmony, he's creating the materials needed to rebuild...

'Course, if he gives people a new form of matter nobody can destroy—if nobody can work it, it's just huge pieces of garbage, man."

Rumble-rumble...!! A sharp, heavy growl shook the snowfield a moment later.

The Academy City man, lying down on the cot, sat up, wincing in pain. The Russian soldier receiving aid the next cot over did the same.

"Damn it. Give me a gun," groaned the man, reaching out for a nun. "I won't sit by and wait for them to do us in. I don't know who you are, but you're good people—good enough to repay in full. I'll buy you enough time to escape, at least."

But the Academy City agent and the Russian soldier wouldn't have to mount a suicide charge.

They hadn't even been given that much time.

Truly, it happened in an instant.

Skkrrr!!

A very long katana severed the golden arm at its base.

Through the gap in the cloth of the simple tentlike shelter, they saw the majestic scene unfolding outside.

The Asian woman swinging around a katana two meters long was certainly remarkable, but the golden arm being torn clean through in a single attack was far more shocking.

The golden arm's length exceeded one hundred meters. Its thickness, too, was similarly massive. No matter how sharp the two-meter katana's blade was, it was a matter of simple thickness—it could never have cut through such a thing.

And yet...

"It's essentially the same logic as cutting open a plastic bag."

They could hear a woman's voice from the card communicator stuck to the wall.

"After making a small wound to the target, you leave it up to the target to tear open a hole on its own. Legends from all over the world, past and present, depict people splitting open evil dragons and the like

that are clearly too big for their swords—this is an essential property for those stories."

A black-clothed nun aimed an old-fashioned light source—an oil lantern, maybe—onto the baffled Academy City man's body. A circular flashlight-like light crawled over him. He thought she was checking him for injuries, but something wasn't right. Even after the circle of light left part of his skin, the surface of his body glowed faintly.

As though supporting his body from the outside.

"Whether you wish to survive or to confront a powerful enemy, we must first create an environment in which you can move your body to your satisfaction."

As he was cared for, the Academy City man remembered what the snowfield outside the shelter was like.

Thinking about where the still-usable tanks and powered suits had been left, as accurately as he could.

In moments, his sortie preparations would be complete.

And this time, his enemy would not be the Russian forces.

Meanwhile, two swords chopped through a giant golden arm that had sprouted from the ground.

The first was a sword of light, extending from a fragment of the British sword, the Curtana Second. The second was a French sword, the Durandal.

Wielding them were representatives of each nation: the second princess, Carissa, and the Femme Fatale. The wounds they had sustained while facing the archangel Misha Kreutzev hadn't healed, but sharpness of their motions hadn't waned.

"First an angel, now symbols of the right arm? He really has a thing for telesma, doesn't he?" Carissa waggled her sword, seeming bored. "Move the mobile fortress *Glastonbury* from point B to point C. And perform a check on it. Can't have it malfunctioning on us now, so."

"...If you could disable the *Glastonbury*'s altitude limiter, you could probably board Fiamma's temple fairly quickly."

The Femme Fatale was looking up overhead. There—over ten thousand meters in the sky—a fortress referred to as the Star of Bethlehem was still raising its altitude.

"We wouldn't be struggling if it was that simple. The *Glastonbury* was developed as a mobile fortress for suppressing land territory, you know. It didn't really have high-altitude aerial combat in mind."

Carissa turned back toward the *Glastonbury*.

Remaining turned around, she muttered.

"...Still, the Star of Bethlehem, eh? I'm surprised the Russian and Roman Churches disclosed the information for it."

"They were being used, just like us. I suppose it simply means they aren't so irredeemable that they'd serve a plan like this in silence."

Shoo, shoo. Lightly spinning her sword with only her wrist, the Femme Fatale thought deeply.

...Come to think of it, I believe my younger sister's independent nation was around here somewhere.

After randomly punctuating her thoughts with a hum, she continued. *If I indebt myself to her now, it may benefit France down the line.*

Wait a minute, Sis. Could one of Europe's representative countries not try to pluck from a small nation? It's puerile.

Oh, Eliza? I do believe it's good manners to at least knock first.

You're in range of my bombardment spell, you know.

I do believe that if you were that talented, the French government wouldn't have let you depart.

We were planning on making that location into an anti-Fiamma battlefield, so my troops have planted all sorts of dangerous things there. In the end, Fiamma invaded before we could use them and stole Sasha Kreutzev in the process. In any case, if it's that location alone, the bombardment spell will reach.

Do you mean to indebt me to you?

I should think a smaller nation plucking from one of Europe's representative countries is the more natural course, wouldn't you?

Crackle-crackle. Sparks flew between the sisters.

And Carissa seemed to have gotten a communication as well.

However, hers wasn't a magical one. The second princess had reacted to a beep, taking out a radio hidden in her chest.

The Femme Fatale looked at Carissa like she was wearing a vulgar swimsuit. "...I keep saying this, over and over and over, but do you *really* need to keep things in there?"

"Quit your prattling. What are you, my mother? ...Unfortunately, my dress doesn't have any sort of pockets. And between this and putting them in my panties, I actually think I'm being rather sensible here, so."

Carissa, having pulled out her radio, seemed to be in contact with London.

"I see, I see. Right. Then to bring down the Star of Bethlehem, we'll need to provide technology and information from the English Puritan Church as well."

She nodded to herself several times.

"Then tell the leader of the Puritans this. If you don't give them the necessary information at once, the Royals' second princess, Carissa, military might of the nation, will shove this Curtana so far up your ass—"

After saying what she needed to, Carissa turned off the radio.

"...You heard it. Looks like they're working on pulling it down, but it also looks like the damage will get worse if we just wait around."

"Then there's only one thing to do."

Spitting the words out, the two once again readied their legendary-class swords.

Several golden arms appeared from the ground, surrounding them.

Entrusting their backs to each other, they spoke:

"Even without actually going inside the Star of Bethlehem, there are ways to keep Fiamma from getting what he wants, so."

"...Destroying every last one of the golden arms appearing on the surface, in other words."

Several slashes struck out, and in the blink of an eye, the encirclement collapsed.

The men of the Knights, as well as Necessarius and the French sorcerers, followed after them.

Their invasion had begun.

At the same time, in St. George's Cathedral in Britain, a slim western sword made of what looked like particles of light ripped into the sorcerer Stiyl Magnus, slashing him from his shoulder to his breast. The sword of Freyr, god of fertility. Moving on its own, the Soul Arm would always slash the opponent's vital spots, and it had just torn Stiyl's clavicle and ripped through thick arteries and internal organs.

The expression on the girl named Index remained still.

Stiyl's movements stopped.

And even then, multiple attacks continued.

Two more swords stabbed into Stiyl's waist and back, and as if to land the finishing blow, the bloodred wings swung down—an utterly hopeless, overwhelming attack. A combo that, as it crushed every bit of his human flesh, also dealt fatal damage to his life force, the wellspring of mana.

However.

The expressionless Index then tilted her head slightly to the side.

The swords and wings had certainly slid inside Stiyl's body. That, however, was the only change. It had happened too smoothly. No blood spilled, and no flesh crushed. Human bodies couldn't be cut apart like a spoon going through yogurt.

Her judgment lapsed for a moment.

And by the time she realized it was a product of sorcery, the next thing had happened.

"A mirage. A common trick."

A voice from behind her.

An odd feeling on her back.

A moment later, there was the *zhh-bang!!* of an explosion that sounded like a lightning strike. Stiyl had demonstrated the full power of the binding cards he'd pasted all over.

Creeeeeeaaaaak!!!!!! Index's spine arched and cracked.

"Warning. Chapter 47, Verse 80. Confirmed psychosomatic binding effect due to psychological effects. Affecting cognitive faculties. Guiding binding effect toward dummy region and prioritizing the securing of the ability to back-calculate spell."

Starting from the side that'd been triggered, the runes inscribed on the laminated cards began to fade, like posters left in the sunlight too long. The coloring, an important matter for runes, was beginning to be undone. Naturally, when the color was gone, the effects would end. They wouldn't hold for long.

…The remote-control Soul Arm's intervention is weakening her, but she's still a library of 103,000 grimoires. I doubt this will be enough to seal her.

All Stiyl Magnus could do was buy time.

On a fundamental level, he could not beat Index.

However.

"That doesn't matter."

Stiyl smiled a little, taking new rune cards out of his inside pocket.

"If that detestable man finishes things in the meantime, we'll have won."

Click. He heard the sound of a footstep.

He looked that way and saw Laura Stuart smiling.

She was waggling something she was holding in her hand.

Stiyl was stunned, at first thinking it was the remote-control Soul Arm—but it wasn't.

What she was holding was a card-shaped communication Soul Arm.

"Reward for you," she said.

The Roman Orthodox Church and the Russian Catholic Church.

While bringing her lips to the communication Soul Arm connected to each of their leaders…

"Well! It looks like you've filled your quota, so I, too, will do my very darndest to recover the library of grimoires."

And so:

The English Puritan Church, the Roman Orthodox Church, and the Russian Catholic Church.

The three greatest denominations of Crossism had finally joined forces.

To strip power away from Fiamma of the Right's fortress, the Star of Bethlehem, and stop any further atrocities.

Together, they broke the chains binding the world and began to act.

Touma Kamijou and Fiamma of the Right each swung around his "arm."

Several shock waves rattled their surroundings, the magical after-effects turning into a flood of light and scattering nearby. Aside from the direct collisions, light sporadically flickered around them, bloodred rays firing in multiple directions. These were attacks utilizing the 103,000 grimoires.

However, their clash was not even.

Little by little, like a sharp beak picking away at meat, with every collision the strength drained from Fiamma's third arm. He could tell that his arm, for which he had obtained special flesh and blood through various rituals, was crumbling into dust.

It wasn't that Kamijou's power was special.

The source of the power supporting Fiamma of the Right was just steadily breaking.

Why? wondered Fiamma.

His third arm, which was supposed to have incredible strength, was rapidly losing output. As for the Star of Bethlehem, which he'd put together using the essential parts of churches and cathedrals from around the world, it was cracking here and there, and it had lost its original shine. And no matter how much time passed, he was unable to bring the surface, which was supposed to alter in the same way as the golden sky, under his control. Far from it—in fact, small, dull stains had appeared in a few places in the field of gold. Something was wrong. It seemed stopping one cog's rotation had hindered the motion of every single other part of the mechanical contrivance.

Nothing was going as he wanted it to.

At this rate, he wouldn't be able to keep up.

His power's emission had grown larger than its supply, and that would result in Fiamma weakening.

"Oooooooooooooooooooooooooooooooooohhhhhhhhhhhhhhhhh hhhhhhhhhhhhhhhhhhhhhhhhhhhhhhhhhhhhhhhhhhhhhhhhh!!!!!!"

Fiamma, screaming, exercised his third arm faster and with even more strength.

But he himself had realized the action was contradictory. His arm was all-powerful to begin with. If he swung it, it would hit—he didn't need speed. If he struck, he would crush, so he didn't need to seek force, either. Despite that, Fiamma was relying on his shallow arm strength. Proof that the "essence" supposedly residing in that arm was wavering.

Bu-boom!! came a low shaking.

The entire Star of Bethlehem was rumbling. But it wasn't because of Kamijou and Fiamma's battle. This quaking was completely isolated. The very fortress was about to experience a collapse.

The fortress's speakers turned on by themselves.

Fiamma didn't know this, but the voice belonged to a girl named Lesser.

"The English, Roman, and Russian Churches have begun disengaging the spells on the Star of Bethlehem's joints! Once me and—um, the Russian Church's Sasha Kreutzev have embedded a relay point for the disengagement spell, we're getting into an escape container. There are barely any containers left! You need to hurry, too, please!!"

Once again.

An irregular, one that Fiamma of the Right hadn't even considered, had struck a blow to his plans.

A factor by the name of *goodness*.

"It's over, Fiamma," said Kamijou quietly, readying his right fist. "The core of your plan, your right arm, is losing power. Your ritual site, the Star of Bethlehem, will be useless soon. And most importantly, if you'd really wanted to save the world, you would have been *happy* that the goodness in people's hearts won out over the evil... And since you can't be happy about it, that means your illusions have already broken down."

"You may be right."

Fiamma chuckled.

"I'm at a disadvantage in this situation. If that essential power is diminished, my grand plan cannot continue. My purification of the surface has stalled as well...Even if I swing this right arm, losing power as rapidly as it is, I wouldn't even be able to take the surface with me. At this rate, everything will be brought to nothing."

"..."

"At this rate anyway."

They were ominous words.

And then—

Wham!! The golden skies overhead swayed. Shading appeared in its glow. Then, all at once, a mass of light headed for the Star of Bethlehem. Clumps of energy, produced one after the next, taken in, compressed into the fortress's interior.

As Kamijou's expression changed, Fiamma shook the remote-control Soul Arm a little. "I didn't use this, just so you know. This is something all of *you* caused."

"What...?"

"I couldn't get anyone's support, but *time* has taken my side," Fiamma explained.

He wasn't going to open the door to Heaven. The world around him had turned into something incredibly sacred, and he would remake it in Heaven's image.

The changes progressed over time until they crossed the line.

"Originally, the surface was supposed to change, too, a little at a time, in stages. But because your so-called goodness has refused that at every turn, like continental plates bending and building power, the lot of you have created unnatural distortions between the skies and the surface."

Even now, huge quantities of energy were pouring into the Star of Bethlehem. Once it exceeded its capacity, he wouldn't be able to hold back the buildup any longer.

"And as a result, enormous swaths of power are descending from the telesma-filled skies to the telesma-less surface like a flowing electric current…It's honestly not the route I had in mind, but as long as the earth is filled with that light, it changes nothing. This world's transformation will continue."

"You understand what's happening?" said Kamijou through clenched teeth. "It's a huge chunk of energy, like for making an angel body. If something like that falls to the surface, it won't just be a transformation—there's gonna be an insane explosion covering the whole map!! It was the same with Misha during Angel Fall. If that level of power goes out-of-control crazy, it could wipe out human civilization as we know it!!"

"That's right—it's certainly too bad. For you anyway. Judging by how much power it is, it'll at least engulf the entire Eurasian continent in its light."

A fire still flickered in the lights of Fiamma's eyes.

This was the first time the phrase *Never give up* had come across in such a wicked fashion.

"A little *goodness* may have sprouted during this war, but this overwhelming destruction will blot it out from above. Now you realize it was all for naught, that brandishing your *goodness* could not stop this tragedy. And the hopelessness of that realization will change into something far deeper, far heavier than the evil that was around from the start."

And that highly dense mass of evil borne of resignation would whet the power within Fiamma. Even more than before. Even more strongly than what Fiamma had predicted. He would stand at the pinnacle of all things living on this planet, wield his power however he wished, and transform the world.

"The colossal divine punishment will easily raze the trifling unity of humanity. Just as the Tower of Babel's destruction split apart human bonds. It will create evil, and I will respond to that, once again able to draw forth incredible power."

"...Fiamma..."

"You were too late to save the world by your methods," he declared, smiling, as Kamijou gripped his fist tighter than he had ever before.

It was a comforted smile, one borne from having leeway—of a supply of immense power guaranteed.

"And now, I have won."

INTERLUDE EIGHT

After stuffing a piece of cloth into a small, window-like depression in the Nu-AD1967's warhead side, Mikoto finally heaved a sigh.

"*Hff...hrff...*Well, *that* better have disabled this warhead. If they start using all sorts of ultrasonic stuff, I'm going to be in trouble."

"Judging from the chaos in their communications, they do not appear to have any further measures, reports Misaka. They seem significantly confused that nothing is happening, adds Misaka, appending emotional information."

"Think they'll come out with another plan?"

"Now that they've lost their implementation unit, they seem to be moving into a retreat, guesses Misaka. Because they don't have the power left to carry a warhead of this size, they appear to be abandoning the nuclear weapon, Misaka also offers, listening in on the details."

"Still, if we leave this here, I bet we'll have trouble later."

"...That seems to be what a separate faction in the Russian forces has decided as well, and a special forces team has surrounded the officers, reports Misaka, intercepting another communication. It seems they will engage them as they leave the building with a 'special suppression operation,' finishes Misaka."

"Maybe they're not stepping right into the building to give them a false sense of security and not give them a reason to set off the nuclear bomb. They can't ignite it right away from inside a vehicle, after all."

Mikoto pushed the end of a shovel, which she'd had the Sister throw to her, into the spot above where the cloth was shoved in. It had been attached to a tank body. Mikoto, controlling electromagnetic forces, shattered the reinforced glass around the light receiver.

"Then it'll be over if I bust the warhead connectors."

After destroying three more spots that connected to its computer, Mikoto turned back to the Sister.

"Okay, it's over. Now the warhead's useless. Unless they put it in a different shell anyway."

"The warhead alone weighs two tons, so they most likely cannot carry it without a crane, estimates Misaka."

"Just to be sure, I'll give Russian authorities or Academy City a tip to help them find this place."

With that, the issues regarding the nuclear weapon were solved.

Now it could start.

The real show would finally begin.

Mikoto Misaka hadn't come to Russia to do something like this. She'd come here so she could see that spiky-haired idiot and give him a piece of her mind in the form of a punch to the face.

She spun around, taking in her surroundings. "You come installed with the ability to handle weapons, right?"

"If necessary, I can also obtain additional information from the Misaka network, says Misaka offhandedly, while conversing with the other individuals regarding how to proceed with negotiations for part-time pay."

"Can't pay anyone high school or younger, so you're working for free."

Ignoring the Sister as she muttered *Are you not getting your priorities wrong in several ways?* Mikoto pointed in a certain direction.

"I don't know if they wanted more air combat power or a means of transportation, but there's a VTOL over there. We could fly to that fortress in the sky if we used it, couldn't we?"

CHAPTER 12

Final Battle in the Arctic Ocean

Last_Fight.

1

The white snowfield was veiled in silence.

Accelerator had stopped singing. The tip of his crutch, supporting his body off the ground, slipped out. He buckled at the knees, covered head to toe in scarlet blood. In that white hell that denied even color, he alone gave off some of his own, borne of his wounds and pain.

Ragged breaths escaped him, scraping against his weary throat like sandpaper. His exhalations occasionally brought red fluid out with them, his body damaged even on the inside.

He couldn't sing any longer.

Something sticky was glued to all the tubes in his body.

However.

His lips, stained dark red, were loosened in a subtle smile. *That's right*, he thought. *I don't have to sing anymore. Because…*

"Are…you okay…? asks Misaka asks Misaka."

In his hazy vision, he heard a small voice.

The voice of a girl that he'd wanted to hear for so, so long. The words of a girl who hadn't even been allowed to stay conscious until just now, who hadn't had even a minimal guarantee that she would live. When he heard that voice, Accelerator had regained a little of his core—he was sure of it.

It flickered, maybe ready to disappear at any moment—a terrifyingly unreliable thing. But he knew that a pillar was placed in its center now, one that would last forever.

Last Order was finally stable.

She'd never have to suffer through this unreasonable violence ever again.

Accelerator ruminated deeply on this truth. And before he knew it, he was moving. That Level Five, once called the strongest monster in Academy City, reached out with trembling hands and embraced Last Order's little body, still limp, devoid of energy.

Tightly.

So that they would never part again.

"...I'm glad..."

The words escaped him softly, his voice shaking.

And not only because his insides were so torn up.

"Shit. I'm so fucking glad...!!"

Those words may have never come from the true Accelerator.

But how was he able to say which was the true one? Couldn't this also have been his true self? Before all these tragedies had begun, before Academy City's darkness had swallowed up a young Level Five, wasn't the *true* him a child who had laughed like every other, who had cried like every other?

Even as all that evil had permeated him, *that* was inside him, unchanged.

It had been there the whole time.

Maybe this was what Kikyou Yoshikawa and Aiho Yomikawa had seen—and what they'd tried to keep safe within a society of adults.

Last Order, who had for a long time only been occasionally conscious, wouldn't have known any of the details of these events.

But that didn't matter.

As he hugged her, she put her little hands around Accelerator's back and slowly rubbed it.

As if to accept him.

In the same way, probably, as she had when she'd been the first to find what had remained inside him.

"..."

As he felt her finally regain warmth, Accelerator turned inward to think.

This world was cold, harsh, and filled with a hopeless amount of evil.

But there was salvation, too.

If you reached out with your own will. If you gritted your teeth and kept moving forward. At the end of endless, endless struggles, there would always be light. And this world wasn't so hopeless that it would steal even that last ray of hope.

"Sorry for raining on your big, emotional reunion, but..."

Then it happened.

Misaka Worst, who was nearby, spoke in a tone with a thorn of caution in it.

"With the way things are going, this bullshit war probably ain't gonna have a happy ending."

Before Accelerator could turn his neck to check his surroundings, he felt something wrong.

It bolted down his back with a shudder.

An awful sensation, like something cold had entered his entire body through his skin. Except, no, that was backward. The trembling was from inside him, escaping onto his skin.

Either way, though, his five senses weren't acting normally. This had to do with his body's sensors, or his brain's calculation circuits were malfunctioning because he'd forcibly taken information he shouldn't ever have.

He felt an immense pressure from directly above.

Mitsuki Unabara, the angel of water, the parchment. Whatever those things gave off, this was like a far more concentrated version...

Still embracing Last Order, Accelerator cast his gaze to the skies.

The giant fortress was floating there.

Golden light covered the skies, steadily engulfing the fortress. The pressure of an enormous force, all converged on one point, sent a tingling sensation through Accelerator's skin. He sensed its aim. That strange mass of power was targeting the surface.

He didn't know what that fortress represented.

Nor did he understand what sort of effects it would bring when the power hit the surface.

But...

"...Nothing good's gonna happen if that thing fires."

Its goal may not have been only pure destruction. It might produce some sort of special effect. But the result was the same. If that much power fell to the ground, how far would the damage spread? Plus, if he followed the feeling on his skin and assumed it was a different sort of energy than a purely scientific force, his reflection wouldn't work on it.

If it penetrated that, everyone would die.

Accelerator, Misaka Worst, Last Order...Every single person.

"...That's a load of bullshit."

It happened a moment later.

Boom!!!!!!

With an explosive sound, wings, jet-black like ink, spurted from Accelerator's back.

The black wings that symbolized his anger.

A massive power wrapped in an enigma: It didn't seem like something simply borrowed from the Misaka network, and it was unclear whether Last Order could force it to stop. In fact, when these wings had appeared, Accelerator himself was almost always in a state where he'd lost his mental balance. When he wanted so badly to kill the enemy before him that he'd abandon all sense of principles, of who he was. The killing intent bursting out from within his chest violated the world in the form of black wings. An incorrigible power.

It was almost like the pressure from the celestial fortress had squeezed them out of his body.

Just like when he'd fought Aiwass.

However.

"...Misaka Worst." His words were a whisper. "I'll go stop that thing. Can I get you to protect the kid?"

"From Russia? Or from Academy City?"

"From everything."

Misaka sighed at the unreasonable command. Turning against both sides was like telling her to fight the combined forces of everyone in World War III.

But when she gave him a grin filled with malice, she took an iron spike out of her pocket and said, "...Well, we were already gonna make them pay for this, so I guess it's all the same. And if we analyze Last Order and the data for the song in the Misaka network, it might grace us with a chance to obtain technology that doesn't exist in Academy City."

Last Order, perhaps uneasy with how dizzying these developments were, latched on to Accelerator's clothes. "Where are you going? asks Misaka asks Misaka."

Her eyes wavered as she looked up at him from his arms.

She probably knew what Accelerator was about to attempt. And because she knew, she was trying to stop him.

"You're not going anywhere, right? says Misaka says Misaka, getting confirmation and stuff."

"Nothing to worry about. It'll be over soon," said Accelerator, not mentioning if he'd ever return, if he'd ever come back home.

The monster who had sprouted black wings gently released the girl's fingers that were clutching his clothing, one by one, as if to throw off the last fetters still keeping him on the surface.

"No!" came Last Order's weak voice. "I want to be with you forever, says Misaka says Misaka."

"...Yeah."

Accelerator, too, admitted it.

At the very end, he gave a cherubic smile and answered:

"I wanted to be with you forever, too."

Crack-crack-crackle-crackle!! With a sound like ice breaking, the color of the monster's wings began to change. From a deep ink-black to an immaculate snowy white. From their roots to their tips,

in mere instants, everything—from its outer coloring to its inner essence—began to be replaced.

Just above his head, a small ring of the same color appeared.

This was how he had changed.

How his mind, the wellspring from which his singular power gushed forth into this real world, had altered.

Accelerator placed his hands on Last Order's tiny shoulders and gave her a soft push. Like an astronaut in zero gravity, the recoil caused his body to float gently into the air.

Last Order's small hands reached toward the man in the air.

But they didn't reach.

Accelerator was already floating several meters high.

This was the right thing to do.

Convinced of that, Accelerator flapped his pearly wings. They were giant, reaching hundreds of meters in length, and they didn't change mere wind force into lift but, instead, had a much stranger energy: They applied zero force to the surface, and yet, his body shot straight up like a cannonball.

In the blink of an eye, he ascended three thousand meters, scattering the edges of the thick clouds about to cover up the skies.

The aerial fortress moved at the same time.

A mass of golden energy, taken from above and accumulated on its lower part, dropped without mercy. He felt the sort of pressure that sent people's spines tingling. As he'd thought, it, like Accelerator's white wings, was not a normal power. His reflection probably wouldn't affect it, either. Reflection's power would penetrate it, just like when Aiwass had defeated him.

But so what?

Accelerator worked his white wings even more, skyrocketing his ascension speed. He headed straight for that falling golden mass without using any tricks. There was even a subtle smile on his lips.

I get it, thought Accelerator belatedly.

This *is what it's like to fight to protect something.*

*   *   *

A moment later, at an altitude of eight thousand meters, two enormous forces collided.

2

Whu-whuuuump!!!!!! A tremendous impact rocked the Star of Bethlehem.

There was an explosion of golden light.

"What…?"

However, the great calamity Fiamma of the Right expected to assault the earth never came to pass. And the surface was never steeped in the same gold as the skies. Some other factor had stopped the large-scale telesma that was dropped from the Star of Bethlehem.

"It should have had enough output!! Destruction enough to fulfill my strategic objective on the surface should have assured my victory!! What in the world…?!"

The tragedy he'd hoped for hadn't happened.

Malice's amplification went unrecognized, with the tragedy instead having been held in check—and thanks to that, the dark parts of people's hearts were starting to be wiped away.

Perhaps it was no more than temporary, like the feeling of oneness with the world only felt during sporting festivals, the heat of wild excitement.

However.

Even if for no more than an instant, those on the surface must have thought this.

This world is doing fine with just us.

Your condescending salvation can fuck off.

"You good now?"

Touma Kamijou, fist clenched, took a step forward.

One step. Two steps. Three steps.

"It's about time for your illusions to call it quits."

With a *booooooom!!!!!!* he turned his steps into a run, all at once.

Kamijou didn't need any silly tricks. All he'd do was get close, fair and square, as close as he could. In response, Fiamma of the Right swung the symbol of his power, his third arm, with all his might. Even the Imagine Breaker wouldn't be able to cancel out the enormous power packed inside. If he failed to divert its path, it would be able to pulverize his entire right arm. Perhaps that was what Fiamma thought when he used brute force to try to eliminate the obstacle before his eyes.

But Kamijou didn't stop.

As soon as he rammed his right fist squarely into the oncoming third arm, Fiamma's greatest weapon, that malformed arm, was squarely blown away.

Fresh blood and flesh danced.

His third arm, which had finally gained flesh, lost its vessel, shaking in agony in midair.

"Wha...what?!" cried Fiamma, face warping, as though an unknown and intense pain had slammed into him like an avalanche.

It wasn't that Kamijou's power had been increased or anything. The Imagine Breaker was still only the Imagine Breaker.

Fiamma's third arm, which responded to malice, had weakened to the point where even the Imagine Breaker could destroy it. As a result of that small goodness rippling out to cover the surface, the shaft supporting Fiamma's power had broken.

The power that made Fiamma of the Right special no longer existed.

Indirect forms of attack from the third arm were unlikely, of course—but so was his evasive maneuver that instantly moved him kilometers away in a horizontal direction.

And now, nothing stood in the way of Touma Kamijou's advance.

"Shit...!!"

Fiamma thrust Index's remote-control Soul Arm in front of him. He tried to use the knowledge in the 103,000 grimoires to intercept the approaching Kamijou. He felt a terrible, stabbing headache, as though his defenses had weakened, too, upon losing his special power, but he ignored it and continued to search the knowledge base. His eyes were a declaration that he'd kill the enemy before him no matter what it took.

But then Fiamma heard a voice.

It belonged to what he was supposedly magically connected to—the library of grimoires.

…Warning. Chapter 88, Verse 1. Anomaly detected in currently searching main body. Excess of external stimulation has caused a serious reduction in search efficiency.

"…?!"

The index's main body was supposed to be in safekeeping in St. George's Cathedral. If external stimuli had caused an error, then an English Puritan sorcerer must have done something.

His final option was totally cut off.

This was the difference between the two.

The decisive difference between one who had only polished his power to stand alone at the peak and one who had struggled to stand at that peak through the help of others.

The small, unimportant high school student tightened his right fist and ran toward the king manipulating the world.

Deeply.

Sharply.

All the way to a throne that had never let any others near it.

And then it happened.

Slllppp…!! Kamijou's feet suddenly sank.

The Star of Bethlehem was weakening.

Its power source from Fiamma of the Right severed, it had naturally begun to collapse.

At the very, very end, something had stopped Touma Kamijou.

And it was called…

Rotten luck.

Fiamma's lips twisted eerily.

He focused his mind on the remote-control Soul Arm in his hand one more time.

Five, ten seconds—that's all I need. That's long enough for me to rewire the grimoire library's settings!! I don't care if the high load burns out the 103,000 volumes. I will wash away this enemy before me right now!!

"Oo—"

However.

Touma Kamijou's forward march didn't stop there.

The boy shouted and plunged ever onward.

"—ooooooooooooooooooooooooooooooooooooooooooooohhh hhhhhhhhhhhhhhhhhhhhhhhhhhhhhhhhhhhhhhhhhhhhhhhh!!!!!!"

Bam!!

With a boom, Kamijou jumped from his nearly crumbled foothold.

To cross the fissure separating the two.

Forward, toward Fiamma—like an arrow.

And then Fiamma knew.

He knew what sort of being this "enemy" before his eyes fundamentally was.

Are you…kidding me…?

Index's remote-control Soul Arm wouldn't make it.

This enemy wouldn't even give him that little bit of time.

I'm using the miracles and blessings of Jesus at their full capacity and causing all sorts of phenomena—and this bastard doesn't care?! It has nothing to do with good or bad luck—this fool has the power to personally trample over all such ambiguities…!!

"If you don't think you can save anyone without doing things this way…"

The words came from deep within Touma Kamijou. Uniting those raging emotions together, he put all his strength into his right fist.

"…then first, I'll destroy that illusion!!"

A thundering boom rang out.

Fiamma, who had never received an attack from anyone, was knocked down with sheer momentum by a punch to the face.

The vestiges of the third arm, still trying to cling to this world, vanished completely this time, melting into the air.

At the same time.

From his hand fell the remote-control Soul Arm that had been manipulating Index.

3

Fiamma of the Right's loss of the third arm visited major aftereffects on his floating fortress as well. Greater shaking was happening frequently now, inviting more unrest than before. The fortress's ascent had stopped dead, having still been continuing until now. The source of its flotation of this much matter was steadily being lost. At this rate, it would eventually start to descend. Escaping before that was probably the only way to live.

On the ground, Fiamma looked at his own hand.

The remote-control Soul Arm was gone.

When he'd been punched, the impact had wrested it from his hand. It had fallen somewhere through one of the cracks in the floor. It was likely still inside the fortress, but he had no idea where it would have gone.

If only he had that, maybe he would have been able to counterattack with normal magic, he thought.

But he didn't have any strength left in his limbs. Now that he'd lost the third arm, he was no different from a mere human. Even a light concussion would be enough to stop him from moving.

In his hazy consciousness, he heard a voice.

It was from the speakers set up all around the Star of Bethlehem.

"We didn't have time, so me and—er, Sasha, was it?—and I…Anyway, we went ahead and used a container to escape. Please hurry. The Star of Bethlehem is going to start falling soon. The fortress itself is falling apart, and there are only so many usable containers left."

He could see the fortress's lowest level beyond the broken floor. And that was only a few layers of overlapping metal grating; the very bottom was connected to open sky. Escape containers hung from it, too, but most were unusable now. Some containers had been crushed, while the lowering hooks on others had broken and were now inoperable.

There was probably only one usable container left.

It was swaying unreliably and only about the size of a public phone booth. Not one of the larger containers that could carry over fifty people at once. Only one person would be able to ride it. Having lost his third arm and becoming a normal person, Fiamma couldn't even get himself down from this altitude by his own power.

Touma Kamijou and Fiamma of the Right.

Which would go aboard the container, and which would perish along with the fortress?

The question didn't even warrant consideration.

...*So this is it.*

That was all Fiamma thought.

If every human living in this world would refuse salvation, it didn't matter to him anymore. They could follow their chosen path and hurtle toward extinction for all he cared.

Slowly relaxing his entire body, Fiamma closed his eyes.

And then someone grabbed his collar.

"Hey, we're going."

It was Touma Kamijou.

Forcing Fiamma upright, his own body covered in blood, he began to walk, dragging the limp villain behind him.

"...What...are you doing...?"

"We don't have time. The Star of Bethlehem is starting to fall. If we don't escape before then, we'll be stuck here."

"Do you not understand the situation?" accused Fiamma in his puppet state. He used his jaw to gesture toward where they were going. "The escape containers are unusable. At most, there's one good one meant for one person. It's me or you. It'll only help one of us."

"Looks like it."

Kamijou exhaled once.

So he said, "Then you escape. Either way, there's no time. Let's get there fast."

"..."

This time, Fiamma looked up at the side of Kamijou's face, dumbfounded.

In the meantime, still dragging him along, Kamijou went down to the lowest floor and headed for the escape container.

He was serious. There was no need to posture at this stage in the game. If he abandoned Fiamma, the cause of all this, and climbed into that escape container, he could return alive. He'd be a hero, acknowledged by everybody. Nobody would criticize him for letting Fiamma die. In fact, many would doubtlessly *praise* him for delivering the finishing blow to the mastermind who caused so much tragedy.

And yet.

Why did he say those words now?

No matter how much he thought about it, Fiamma couldn't find an answer. And in that time, they arrived in front of the escape container. Kamijou, with much trepidation, reached for the container door. His right hand's power didn't destroy the container.

After opening the door, he unflinchingly stuffed Fiamma's body inside.

This guy was insane.

He tried to get out of the container, but being so gravely injured, his body couldn't move.

Automatically, he shook his head.

Even he didn't know what he was trying to reject.

"…Are you sure…?"

"About what?"

"I have no idea how large this world you talk about really is."

"Oh," said Kamijou, smiling a little.

Why had he smiled? Fiamma couldn't understand.

"Then now's when you start getting out there and seeing everything you can."

The escape container's door was locked from the outside. A moment later, the container slid along a short rail before being tossed into the open sky.

For a while, Kamijou watched the container as it fell and grew smaller.

Eventually, he shook it off and peered up.

The final container had launched.

There was no longer any way for him to safely escape this fortress.

And then it happened.

There was a thunderous boom. The raging winds changed direction. Kamijou, having unconsciously covered his face with his arms, spotted a fighter jet. It was called a VTOL, an aircraft that could ascend vertically like a helicopter and stop in midair.

He knew the face of the person riding in the cockpit.

It was...

4

"More to the right!! ...Little more!! Get a little closer!!"

Mikoto Misaka, leaning out of the rear seat, shouted at the Sister operating the flight yoke.

Finally.

After all this time, finally.

She'd finally reached the same time and space as that idiot!!

"Big Sister, your face is eerily smiley, indicates Misaka."

"*Bfuh?* That's not true!! And you're just comparing me to yourself, which is messing up your judgment!!" said Mikoto, hastily pulling on her cheeks to check. She continued, "Argh! What the heck is even happening?! It was floating up there just fine until a minute ago. Why did it decide to start falling *now*?!"

"Misaka's apologies for interrupting your excitement, but if you don't open the cockpit canopy, your voice will never reach, indicates Misaka."

"Where is it? Which button?!" asked Mikoto before suddenly having doubts.

They were high up, past ten thousand meters. The outside air was below negative fifty degrees Celsius, the air pressure was very low, and there was little oxygen. Would it be okay for her to open the canopy now?

If she didn't, she'd never reach him. But the elements wouldn't let her open it.

Caught in an incredible dilemma, the Sister, impassively bending her head to listen to something, said, "...Something is strange about how the engine sound is reverberating, reports Misaka."

"?"

"This transmission pattern is for below one atmosphere at negative seven degrees, says Misaka, finishing precise calculations. The exact mechanism is unknown, but despite being at an altitude of ten thousand meters, the outside environment seems set up in the same manner as the surface, reports Misaka, giving her conclusion."

"Meaning..."

"You should be able to open the canopy without a problem, declares Misaka."

A moment later.

The canopy, shaped like a rugby ball cut in half lengthwise, opened right overhead. The Sister must have pushed the button.

Just as she'd said, Mikoto had no trouble breathing. She felt a chill on her skin, but it was a far cry from dozens of degrees below zero.

The Sister, keeping the VTOL slightly tilted, moved it slowly. Not with the nose pointed at the fortress, but vertically...in other words, with the right wing tip approaching it, steadily sidling foward.

Just a few meters left.

Only a multiple of a hundred centimeters.

The fortress was swaying unstably, and the precise distance changed each time.

But it was far closer than she had been when she was hesitating in Academy City.

"This is as close as we can get...," the Sister declared. "Landing may be too much of a problem, says Misaka, tightening her grip on the yoke."

The fighter jet's forward movement stopped dead in midair.

They'd only had a little bit left until they reached the fortress.

"VTOLs are for slowly landing on the surface, explains Misaka. If we were to try to force a landing on the fortress when it is bobbing up and down like this, we run the risk of crashing the underside of the fuselage into it, says Misaka, voicing her concerns."

"What about a wider area? The fortress is gigantic. If we go up some more, we should find an area bigger than a midsize farm."

"The fortress's rumbling itself will not change, so we cannot avoid the risk of crashing no matter where we are, says Misaka, responding with a negatory viewpoint. And even if we were able to land on the fortress, if the plane loses its flight capability, escape would become impossible, says Misaka, frowning."

"Fine, then." The canopy still open, Mikoto reached for her belt buckle. "Keep it as balanced as you can! I'm going out to the wing to pull that idiot up here!!"

Mikoto rose from her seat and crawled toward the wing on all fours.

She felt less fear than she thought, maybe because she could glue her feet to the main wing with magnetic force.

She inched forward.

The distance to the spiky-haired boy closed.

Come on...

Clunk. The fortress gave a major rattle.

Her altitude had decreased.

It didn't feel as stable as before.

The rattling was like...

...the invisible strings holding up the fortress were being cut, one by one.

Come on! Reach!!

The VTOL, its body wobbling around and Mikoto plastered to the main wing, closed in on the fortress a little at a time.

And then:

Her eyes met the idiot's.

The spiky-haired boy seemed confused at the means of escape that had suddenly sprung up. Part of her wanted to yell *What the hell were you planning on doing, stupid?* but now wasn't the time to be sticking to her old ways. She'd scold him until he was dead after this.

After coming to the wing's tip, Mikoto stretched her hand out as far as she could.

Would she reach, or wouldn't she?

Their fingertips drew near, until they almost touched.

However.

Then the boy did something she'd never expected.

He shook his head.

And his hand, which he'd almost reached out far enough, stopped.

Wha…?

Mikoto was dumbfounded, and then the boy's lips moved.

She couldn't hear the words.

But she could read his lips.

There's something I still have to do.

Ga-bam!! The fortress gave a massive jolt. Its descent accelerated even more, and became even more unstable, than before. It was as though a large ball rolling down a hilly road had picked up so much speed nobody could turn it back. She had to retrieve the idiot *now*.

However.

The VTOL suddenly rocked. The aircraft swayed, almost as if it was flying away from the fortress.

"Hey!! What do you think you're doing?!"

"The fortress's shaking has exceeded a threshold, reports Misaka. If we continue our approach, this aircraft may crash into it."

"…!!"

Still plastered to the shaking main wing, Mikoto held out her palm and grabbed hold of nearby magnetic forces.

She'd get him by force if she had to—she didn't care.

Anything would work: a button on his school uniform, a belt buckle. She'd use magnetism to drag the boy up and evacuate him from the fortress.

That was her plan. But in actuality, the thread of magnetism that connected her to him abruptly broke off.

"Huh…?"

Mikoto stared blankly, completely in the dark about what had just happened.

A moment later, though, she understood. The boy had a strange power that canceled out all Mikoto's abilities.

And it had cut off his last lifeline.

Even if she had the power to take on a bunch of tanks at once—even if she had the power to stop a nuclear missile launch.

It wasn't enough to rescue that one boy.

As the fortress continued its unstable descent, the VTOL drew away from it. The Sister pulled Mikoto, who was idle atop the turbulent main wing, into the cockpit and shut the canopy. The blessing of the mysterious field around the fortress was immediately lost.

The reason was simple.

That was how far away they'd gotten.

Leaving the boy, who said he still had something he needed to do, behind in the fortress.

A moment later, the only sound was Mikoto Misaka's scream.

5

...There's still something I have to do.

The VTOL pulled away. The fighter craft that might have been his last way to escape.

But Kamijou had turned his back on it.

His fight couldn't end just yet. The Star of Bethlehem had a radius of over forty kilometers. If a structure this big was in free fall, the damage it would do to this celestial body called Earth would be incredibly severe. The war wasn't over until someone did something about this problem.

And besides...

Kamijou looked around and searched for his objective: the remote-control Soul Arm meant for controlling Index from the outside. It had fallen through a crack in the floor after the last attack. He needed to find it and destroy it.

His footing swayed.

The way it shook made him anxious, like an elevator moving at a fixed speed that suddenly stopped.

This fortress wouldn't hold for long.

And when he realized that again, he heard a girl's voice ringing in his ears.

A voice that couldn't possibly have been there.

"Touma..."

It was the voice he thought he'd wanted to hear for so long.

The remote-control Soul Arm had left Fiamma's hands, but it was probably still working. Her consciousness, no longer suppressed by anyone, was drifting about the space around the Soul Arm.

"Touma..."

Then, faintly...

...her body appeared, translucent, as if rising out of the air. Upside-down and ignoring gravity, she looked at Kamijou's face.

She spoke.

"Why didn't you escape?"

"Because nothing's finished yet," he answered, going farther into the Star. He wasn't searching blindly; her very presence was leading him to the Soul Arm. "Your Soul Arm is still around, of course, but I have to take care of the fortress itself, too."

After saying that, Kamijou's expression suddenly clouded.

There was just one thing he hadn't resolved during his battle with Fiamma of the Right.

"...I'm sorry."

The fact that he had amnesia.

The question of whether hiding it all this time was truly the right thing to do, he simply hadn't wanted to hurt Index. He wanted to be the Touma Kamijou she believed in. But wasn't that only because he personally didn't want to see Index's face in shock? Wasn't he just scared she'd leave him?

Now that he'd finished his fight with Fiamma, he understood:

If he truly thought it was best for her, then he had to overcome.

Overcome the painful, overcome the bitter, overcome everything.

Don't fear the position in which you stand.

"I've done something terrible to you. I've been lying to you all this time. I'm going to tell you everything now. I don't have a guarantee I'll be able to come back from the Star of Bethlehem, so I'll tell you while I still can."

Very slightly, Kamijou looked down.

And then, once more, he lifted his eyes of his own accord.

"I…"

He spoke.

And this…was the first time.

The first time he'd ever felt like this.

Felt like opening his mouth took so much courage.

"I…"

What he'd been hiding from her all this time.

His amnesia.

The truth.

"

                                                                    ."

As he moved his mouth, forming words, he thought, *That was long.*

"It's fine."

He heard Index's voice cutting him off.

"That's all fine now. It doesn't matter. If the same old Touma comes back home, none of it matters."

"…"

For just a moment, he was silent.

He truly wanted to take her up on her kindness.

"I'll come back. I promise."

But being hard on himself and being pessimistic were different things.

He'd live and return for certain.

For that, Touma Kamijou needed to promise this.

"And it won't just be for this Soul Arm. Once I get back, I'll apologize to you for real."

He glanced at a panel on a nearby pillar. It was a communication device fitted with a microphone for broadcasting audio through the speakers all over the Star. He couldn't read the Russian writing, but he did understand the numbers written with them.

"Tell this to the English Puritan Church: The frequency is 50.9 megahertz. That should let them connect to these speakers. If this much matter falls uncontrollably, there's no telling how bad the damage will be. I'll have to lower its speed in stages and set it down somewhere safe. And the only one who can take the wheel right now is me. But I need advice to do it."

"I can't do that." The girl's voice became troubled. *"I can't go back to my body by myself."*

"Didn't think so," Kamijou agreed casually. His eyes settled on that accursed Soul Arm on the floor. "You'll have to go back before me."

He reached out his right hand and grabbed the small, cylindrical Soul Arm.

That was all.

The Soul Arm crumbled into pieces, and at the same time, the power sustaining her was lost. Her translucent body disappeared, too, like an eraser had rubbed it out.

Now he was well and truly alone.

The Star of Bethlehem was still continuing its descent in the meantime. Its speed, too, was steadily increasing. Once it went past the point of no return, it really would crash into the ground at a speed close to free fall.

A direct impact from of a mass over forty kilometers in radius.

If that came to pass, it would demonstrate in twenty-first-century Earth that a meteor collision *had* caused the Ice Age. Some historians might be pleased, but for most people, it would only spell tragedy.

The final battle was about to begin.

As a reward for his gamble, he had been presented with the very fate of this shooting star.

6

"According to information from the Roman and Russian Churches, the Star of Bethlehem floats in the air using twenty large Soul Arms

for levitation. Losing the power from Fiamma has caused its output to drop. At this rate, it will lose all buoyancy after one hour and fall straight down toward the surface."

He could hear Stiyl Magnus's voice emanating from the speakers around the fortress. Kamijou had entrusted him with guarding Index; he'd ended that mission earlier by destroying the remote-control Soul Arm, and now he was guiding Kamijou.

"But if you destroy any of the levitation Soul Arms, we can control the Star of Bethlehem's facing and direction. Meaning your right hand is perfect for the job."

"What exactly should I bust up?"

"Hold on. I just got a map sent to me. It's based on assumptions, so the actual model might be different. If anything seems wrong, report it at once."

Following Stiyl's directions, Kamijou used the facility's monorail, and where he couldn't proceed with that alone, he continued running on his feet. There was no time left anymore. If he failed, six billion lives would be at risk.

"I'll tell you the exact positions by word of mouth, but you'll want to destroy number three, number nine, and number thirteen in the south part. That will cause the Star of Bethlehem's trajectory to change. Have it head for the edge of the Arctic Ocean. We'll drop its speed as much as possible and have it land in the water to prevent the impact. Considering its altitude and mass, that's the only way we won't do massive damage to the planet's environment."

"If we reduce the number of big levitation Soul Arms, won't that make it fall even faster?"

"They share a power source. If there are fewer Soul Arms, that alone will increase the output, one at a time. Of course, it'll be limited to just one at a time, but you don't need to worry about the power supply weakening at the moment. If you thin them out, the output might increase momentarily."

"What are the chances of a tsunami or something if we drop it in the ocean?"

"The cities along the Arctic Ocean's coastline have been warned to

evacuate. *The Roman and Russian Churches are being disgustingly cooperative in helping them. Otherwise, we would have had to be aware of a few casualties."*

In the meantime, Kamijou arrived at the number three Soul Arm. The place looked like a factory.

Large facilities, even bigger than school buildings, lined this enclosed space, with dozens of thick pipes running everywhere. Metal staircases and walkways were a tangled mess between them. Green light particles flitted about intermittently—were they responsible for making this giant fortress float?

Bam!!

Kamijou struck a nearby pipe with his palm.

That was all. With just that, countless cracks formed in the pipe; the square, stone structure tipped over; and brilliant explosions began going off inside it. Kamijou distanced himself to not be caught up in it, then ran toward the next Soul Arm, number nine.

"...Never did I think we'd be fighting side by side in the very end," muttered Stiyl. *"It didn't have to be me. I've been getting sporadic reports from her, too, now that she's finally woken up. Her mind was in the Star of Bethlehem earlier. Couldn't you have solved this situation by relying on her knowledge?"*

"I'm not fooling around here. I couldn't let Index suffer in that state for another minute."

"I get it. It's not my style to owe anything to someone like you, but I'll make an exception this time and accept it."

"If that's really how you feel, could you get a recovery team or something near the projected landing site? I'd really rather not be waiting around in subzero ice water."

"I'll do something about that," answered Stiyl quietly. *"If the gradual descent goes as planned, you shouldn't die even if it lands on the water."*

In the meantime, Kamijou desperately ran through the Star of Bethlehem.

The number nine Soul Arm was right there.

We'll manage, thought Kamijou. This big war that started from a quarrel with the Roman Orthodox Church had been nothing but terrible in every way. But in the end, they'd manage. They'd manage for sure. Confident, Kamijou ran ever forward.

Until...

"What's this...?"

...an impatient voice flew at him from the speakers.

Kamijou listened to it as he ran.

"That's strange. Some kind of massive...telesma? Why would something like that be...?"

He had a bad feeling about this.

But he couldn't stop now. As Kamijou headed for the number nine Soul Arm, Stiyl grumbled:

"Of all the times—why in the hell is Misha Kreutzev surfacing now?!"

7

Concurrently, the archangel who had cooperated with Fiamma of the Right was about to recover its body once again on the wintry Russian lands.

The fluctuations in the four aspects had been corrected by Fiamma's hands. Now, she was not Misha, a mixture of the LIKENESS OF GOD, Michael, and the POWER OF GOD, Gabriel, but an archangel in a pure sense. It would not be a mistake to say that at this point, her goal had, to a certain degree, been accomplished.

But it wasn't enough.

She wasn't *perfect*.

Her goal was simply to return her own existence to its original "seat." Having been about to go off the rails once, she could see no other goal, nor did she consider how much damage would occur in achieving her goal. She would just return. For that, and that alone, the archangel began to move once again.

The massive telesma scattered about her surroundings began to converge toward one point.

She had been torn apart once by the power of the scientific monsters, but they hadn't damaged her essence. Bringing a fist down on water would cause it to splash, but it wouldn't reduce the amount of water itself. It was the same as that.

But it wasn't enough.

She wasn't perfect.

Now that its action had been stopped once, the archangel sought an additional increase in her practical power. She knew well what would serve as material for it. She controlled water. In the winter, Russia had so much snow it covered the ground, but simply melting that wouldn't be enough.

But it wouldn't be enough.

She wasn't perfect.

But it wouldn't be enough.

She wasn't perfect.

But HWSR it wouldn't be enough.

She ZVDF wasn't ZDFB perfect.

BuuuUUUUUUUUUUUUUUUUTTTTTTTTTTTTTTTTTTTT
TTTTTTTTTTTT.

Yes.

To turn around a situation using an overwhelming power, one needed to take all precautions.

A huge amount of ice with special signage and symbolism.

The special ice, for example, from a planet's pole.

"…What is happening…?"

In St. George's Cathedral in London, a Sister around twenty years old let out a moan. She'd been monitoring the flow of magical power in Russia.

"Misha Kreutzev has begun moving northward at a high speed!! The polar ice has also begun to melt extremely quickly!! Additionally—confirmed a massive line of telesma between them!! There is clearly mutual interference occurring!!"

"It wants new power—no, to replenish its body?" Stiyl asked, frowning.

Thinking simply, if that angel had instantly melted all the ice in the Arctic Ocean, phenomena similar to a large-scale tsunami would occur in regions bordering the Arctic Ocean. If the situation progressed too far, an insane water vapor explosion could engulf everything in a radius of thousands of kilometers.

And it wouldn't continue in such a simple manner. If Misha Kreutzev, already brutal, was to take in so much water and ice that it would cause the Arctic Ocean to collapse, how far would her power swell? Now that Fiamma had lost, what was that archangel's objective? Did she not have one at all? They didn't know a single thing, but the endgame she'd create as a result was clear.

They wouldn't be able to withstand it.

In the first place, nothing could contain a God-created angel's full capacity with only matter from the physical world. Even during Angel Fall, Misha Kreutzev hadn't been any more than an incomplete manifestation. If she attempted to forcibly draw out even higher output than envisioned, the body itself composing Misha would explode, equating to a massive discharge of telesma.

A planetary ignition, centered on the North Pole.

At the very least, it would annihilate all living things in the northern hemisphere. In the worst case, it could seriously throw off the actual planet's orbit, possibly pushing it away from the solar system.

But how do we stop it? thought Stiyl, glancing at a magnet that was moving of its own accord on a whiteboard. *I don't know if we could have held back the old Misha even if we fought her as one group. Clashing with an archangel in that wounded state would only magnify the damage.*

Still, if they did nothing, a destructive ending surely awaited them.

And then—

"...Hey, what are you doing?" Stiyl muttered at the screen.

There had been a change in the Star of Bethlehem's flight path, even though it had just been going smoothly. It had begun to travel down a clearly different route than Stiyl and the others' plan. He thought it was a glitch in the fortress, but as far as he could tell from their monitoring, no such trouble had been detected.

Clearly, Touma Kamijou, who was inside it, had done something to a large levitation Soul Arm in an effort to purposely veer it away from the safest route.

In order to block Misha Kreutzev, who was heading for the Arctic Ocean...?

The fortress was falling faster now.

And inside it, Touma Kamijou was running at full speed.

The Arctic Ocean coastline, between sea and land. He'd destroyed a different one of the large levitation Soul Arms to twist the fortress's trajectory that way. In order to stand against the archangel, Kamijou just kept on running.

On the surface, there was a change. Some sort of small shadow was approaching at a high speed.

He could see the snow along the path of whatever it was, shooting along at a low altitude with incredible velocity, being gouged out in enormous chunks. It wasn't simply getting blown away. Hundreds of meters—no, whole kilometers of snow centered around "her" were all getting absorbed at once.

Drawing a long, thick line over the white lands, the archangel headed his way. There was nobody to stop her advance. There seemed to be several along the way who flung magical-looking lights at it, but the archangel didn't even glance their way. She just passed through, mowing down all the professional sorcerers.

The archangel reached the Arctic Ocean from the coastline.

And at the same time...

...The Star of Bethlehem fell directly on top of it.

With an earsplitting *bbb-bbooom!!* the giant fortress fell into the sea along with the archangel. As it sank, Kamijou headed ever downward as fast as he could. Unable to withstand the immense pressure, the walls and pillars inside the fortress collapsed one after another. Severely cold seawater poured inside, but Kamijou didn't pay attention to it. He kept going down. To the bottom. He went below sea level.

There was no more illumination around him.

But there was one speck of light in the expanse of darkness.

A quiet light, deep and blue, reminiscent of moonlight.

Touma Kamijou squeezed his right fist as tightly as he could. She'd noticed him, too. In the dark, only the lights of their eyes clashed a step before they did. As an incredible sense of hostility overflowed, the boy, a simple human, plunged forward, never stopping.

So much had happened before coming here.

And it had all started when he lost his memory. He'd decided to go forward, lying in order to prevent one certain girl's sadness. He'd fought an alchemist to save a girl possessing special "blood." He'd fought the strongest monster, too, to rescue the third-ranked Level Five and her Sisters. At the beach house, he'd fought a death match against a traitor from his class.

A bunch of things had happened on August 31: He'd stood up against a real golem to save a friend, an aggregation of AIM dispersion fields. He'd picked a fight with the largest Crossist denomination to help a Sister professing to be able to decipher the *Book of the Law*. There'd even been an incident related to the Toki-wadai girl's underclassman.

During the Daihasei Festival, even as an executive commit-tee member and a classmate got wrapped up in everything, he'd protected Academy City from the threat of the Croce di Pietro. In Chioggia, Italy, he'd clashed with a fleet of ships made of ice to save a girl who used to be his enemy. On September 30, to save his utterly changed friend, he went head-to-head against a woman from God's Right Seat. The sukiyaki he'd eaten with everyone in his class had been delicious, and he'd run into Skill-Out, too, to help the Tokiwa-dai girl's mother.

In Avignon, France, he'd fought God's Right Seat over the Docu-ment of Constantine. In Academy City's underground city, he'd fought alongside the Amakusa-Style Crossist Church against a powerful saint. In London, England, he'd stopped a coup d'état led by the second princess.

And now.

It's been a long time, he thought.

The things that had transpired up until this point hadn't all been enjoyable.

He'd hurt others, many, many times, and been hurt by others in return, a cycle that had kept on repeating.

However.

Touma Kamijou could still run.

He knew that his actions had saved no small number of people.

He could take on his greatest enemy, this archangel, proudly.

...Maybe this world will be destroyed one day. Even planets have a life span, and I know it'll be swallowed into the sun once it expands. Maybe it's more likely all the creatures will die off the face of the earth before that happens.

But, thought Kamijou, gripping his fist and charging forward.

It's okay for the ending to be less tragic.
It's okay to fight to stop this thing.

With a *boom!!!!!!* the two figures charged at point-blank range.

At the same time, the giant body of the Star of Bethlehem, which had transferred its landing impact in its entirety, was crushed to a pulp.

And.

October 30.

Academy City and the English Puritan Church.

The Roman Orthodox Church and the Russian Catholic Church.

World War III, started by a fight between two factions, ended.

Just before it did, the Star of Bethlehem was confirmed to have fallen into the Arctic Ocean.

Some flood damage was confirmed in cities on nearby coastlines, but not enough to kill anyone.

The very same fortress was completely destroyed by the impact of its landing.

Misha Kreutzev, who had been heading for the Arctic Ocean, had disappeared from all sensors. It was assumed that it had lost the power supporting its existence, disappated into mere energy, and returned to another phase. A stopping of the ice-melting progressing in the same ocean had also been confirmed.

And in that ocean, they detected no survivors.

A search team was dispatched from an alliance of Crossism's three biggest factions, but they never found a survivor in the two-degree-Celsius water.

Touma Kamijou was thus assumed dead.

It was his second death.

EPILOGUE

The Boy and the Stillness
Silent_to_Small_Fire.

"That bastard…," groaned Stiyl Magnus in St. George's Cathedral in London.

He'd gotten the report that the Star of Bethlehem had fallen and had crushed Misha Kreutzev from above. But no matter how big a mass it was, he doubted mere physical pressure would defeat a true angel. As it collided, he'd probably brandished his right hand and fought the monster.

And when Stiyl thought about it, wasn't that the way that man had always done it?

To save the one girl named Index, hadn't he broken free of all chains, stepping forward without hesitation, even taking a hit hard enough to make him lose his memories?

The air in the cathedral was heavy, a far cry from the clamor of a victory celebration. Only businesslike reports continued—that Misha Kreutzev had vanished, that the four aspects had been reset into their former positions.

Stiyl heard a clatter.

He turned around just as a weary Index was coming over to him. She put a small hand on a stone pillar, her steps wobbling, her eyes on the whiteboard.

"Where's Touma?"

It was a question nobody could answer.

Right after Index had awoken in the cathedral, before she could even get up out of bed, she told Stiyl the frequency to connect to the Star of Bethlehem. He doubted anyone had told her what had happened. Maybe the other priests or Sisters couldn't tell her the truth while she was on her way. Finally, Index had come here. To this room, which knew all the results, inside which only a heavy air remained.

She looked around once more, studying the faces of everyone there, and asked again.

"Where's Touma?"

They needed to find something to escape in.

Shiage Hamazura used a thick branch to dig in the snow.

Right before Shizuri Mugino had attacked, the Russian saboteur team had been bombed by an Academy City super-large fighter jet. The vital equipment for the Steam Dispenser and the bacterial wall had been blown away without leaving anything behind, and the saboteur team that was a slight distance away had been neutralized, too, but the vehicles that unit had tried to use to escape must have been caught in the avalanche and buried under the snow.

In the end, he hadn't found anything.

The bacteriological weapon's spray, the battle with number four, the defeat of the Academy City team using weapons "not of this world" and built up using Dark Matter…

At a glance, the results may have seemed so excellent they'd overturn his position as a Level Zero. However, Hamazura and Takitsubo's original objective was to find something that would allow them to negotiate with Academy City's leaders. All they'd done was go onto a side road; they hadn't been getting anywhere down the main street.

They hadn't found a negotiation tool.

If they stayed here like this, they'd be killed.

They needed to leave this place as soon as they could.

Near Hamazura, as he single-mindedly continued digging through the snow, were Takitsubo and Mugino, holding similarly thick branches and doing the same work. Mugino was Academy City's number four Level Five, but after the Crystals and the previous battle, she, too, seemed not to be in a state to use Meltdown right away.

Rewrapping her disheveled scarf, Takitsubo said to him, "Hamazura. What should we do now? Should we pick up the masks the assault team was using and use them as a foothold for a negotiation tool?"

"We'll gather up what we can, but I don't think they'll be enough by themselves. Would they really throw such an Achilles' heel into the middle of enemy lines? That city's darkness runs deep. For them, even letting those masks get out would probably be acceptable."

"Let's use my blood as insurance," piped in Mugino as she continued working with her thick branch. "Number four's DNA map. If we each take a chip with a bloodstain on it, we might have a better chance to throw them off if they split us up."

"...Damn it all."

But Hamazura was looking away from them. He'd stopped digging in the snow, too. He was looking at somewhere far away, it seemed to Takitsubo and Mugino. They moved their heads to follow his gaze.

And then.

There suddenly came the sound of multiple footsteps scattering the snow. Before they knew it, soldiers had surrounded them in a circle about ten meters away. An Academy City kill team, all wearing white from head to toe. Completely indiscernible through their masks and goggles, they gripped carbines in their hands with suppressors attached.

They'd probably been watching Hamazura and the others in a two- or three-layered formation until now.

Considering the people from Academy City's underworld, the extra-large combat forces they'd sent in before now—Shizuri Mugino and the masked men—these attackers were a simple team. Meaning they knew perfectly how exhausted this trio was and had sent in optimal troop strength.

Their time was up.

The moment he realized it, his spirit, inside the body he'd been pushing to its very limits, immediately shattered. In fact, he was envious of Takitsubo and Mugino for still glaring at their enemies with a will to fight blazing in their eyes.

But they would have understood, too.

Rikou Takitsubo and Shizuri Mugino, who had been fulfilling important jobs in Academy City's darkness, had value. It might not be business as usual for them, but there was still room for them to be "retrieved." Hamazura alone, however, was different. Standing on the stage for this long had been absurd to begin with. Even if the higher-ups had chosen the option to take them alive, that would only apply to Takitsubo and Mugino. Hamazura alone would be shot and killed here like a piece of trash.

That was why their eyes displayed such excessive fighting spirit.

He was happy for it.

But at the same time, he realized he was somehow relieved. If he played his cards right, he'd keep sacrifices to a minimum. Not finding a tool to negotiate with the higher-ups was his own fumble, so he swore to stop any more damage. A clear goal had been born within him.

"...Well. You sure have been causing quite a lot of trouble."

A new figure appeared, drawing close to Hamazura and the others as they stood surrounded by ten men. It was a woman with hair the hue of chocolate, wearing an expensive suit. However, ruining the whole image was the full-face helmet she had on. It made her behavior, which spoke to a proper upbringing, appear unnatural instead.

"Although, on the other hand, being able to contain things this much may have proven the strength of our security."

"Who are you?"

"Someone like you," answered the helmeted woman in the suit immediately. "We may even share the same chain of command."

"I recognize the way you talk."

"Oh, please."

At the response, Mugino and Takitsubo exchanged glances. But a shared acquaintance's presence didn't mean they'd let them off the hook, of course. The world wasn't that accommodating.

The woman in the suit continued. "You have a general idea of how you'll be *split up*, I'm sure."

"..."

"We'll immediately recover Shizuri Mugino and Rikou Takitsubo. As for Shiage Hamazura, that's the hard part...Well, the conditions probably don't match. You seem to have built up enough of an interpersonal relationship to use you as a hostage for Takitsubo, but her fundamental movement capabilities are low to begin with. Even without mental shackles, the research can proceed only by isolating her in a concrete room, and if some sort of action was demanded, it would suffice to bury a super-small balloon in her brain, then remotely expand and shrink her cerebral cortex as needed."

"Wait," interrupted Hamazura. "Research? On Takitsubo? Not Mugino?"

"I would guess that those two, at least, have figured it out."

"Figured what out?"

"Shizuri Mugino used Meltdown when you defeated the masked group outfitted with Teitoku Kakine's Dark Matter. But it wasn't that Takitsubo had merely given her verbal instructions. Her Ability Stalker, which interferes with AIM dispersion fields, affected Shizuri Mugino's personal reality, almost forcing her to take aim... Actually, you could go so far as to say she temporarily *overwrote* the correctional information."

He can't mean...Hamazura thought in awe.

He'd heard that Takitsubo had tried something like that in order to fight Teitoku Kakine.

And Shizuri Mugino had possessed Crystals.

"No, that's wrong."

But after studying Hamazura's face, Mugino quickly denied it.

"Takitsubo isn't using the Crystals. In fact, we weren't acting on any sort of operation, either. If we'd had a way to interfere with Level Fives to begin with, her role in Item would have been different...After all, if she could do that, she could strengthen anyone or make anyone go berserk."

The helmeted woman in the suit shrugged and added, "Originally, the plan to make Takitsubo the eighth was independent of the Crystals. The Tree Diagram's simulation results came out, but the real-life conditions were too severe and out of our grasp. That was why we set our sights on Crystals instead, which had a just barely similar effect... Of course, those simulations came out the same: almost completely hopeless."

"...And yet, you still messed with Takitsubo's body."

"Yes, because the chance was just too enticing to pass up. After all, if she continued to evolve and became the eighth, she'd be able to reach through AIM dispersion fields and freely control other espers' personal realities. I'm sure you're not stupid enough to fail to understand what that means."

If such a thing was possible...

The personal reality was the wellspring of every ability and phenomenon in the real world. Controlling it meant a lot more than just increasing or decreasing ability levels. To put it simply, she could give Railgun's ability to Shiage Hamazura and demote Shizuri Mugino to a Level Zero. She could exchange abilities and change their types, too, as she wished. Even the realization of a double esper was a possibility. She could produce all sorts of unsystematic results that ignored affinities and talent.

She could give whatever ability she liked whenever she liked, and take whatever ability she needed wherever she pleased. She could populate a Level Five team for her own convenience, and as for enemy espers, even if it was the number one Accelerator, she could tear his entire personal reality away, disabling him, then kill him.

She'd be far more than the queen of Academy City in that kind of scenario.

There was only one word that could express such a being.

"You see, Rikou Takitsubo...could provide for all of Academy City's functions on her own."

The helmeted woman in the suit gave her answer.

"No—considering she could instantly produce abilities of the desired category and level, and also instantly strip away any unneeded abilities, she would reign as a far more advanced esper-raising machine than Academy City in its current state."

A person with incredible value. So much that it toppled the assumption that there were only seven Level Fives.

"Takitsubo had always had a rare *nature*, but it was difficult to get her to bloom. We dug up the forbidden research from Kihara's cohort and even brought out Crystals knowing the risks, but it wasn't enough stimulation to gain the desired effect…But with this, the pathway to the eighth has opened. Thanks to your wonderful relationship and this terrible war."

As far as Hamazura knew, the only time Takitsubo had seriously tried to interfere with someone else's AIM dispersion field was when the second-ranked Teitoku Kakine had been about to kill him. Did that mean Academy City's leadership had learned from that and purposely let them free to give her an "opportunity" to bloom?

And Takitsubo had obtained a little key.

It was still hard now, but with research, she would become the eighth. Even without the Crystals, she would become a terrifying beast capable of completely controlling the espers all around Academy City.

And she'd do it on her own, with only her one ability.

A being with capabilities that equaled or surpassed all of Academy City's functions as an esper-raising organization.

Instead of Academy City, an Academy Individual.

However.

That wasn't what Shiage Hamazura was most shocked about.

It was pushed down, hidden by the impact of the term *eighth*, but the helmeted woman in the suit had said something he couldn't overlook. Something that, despite being a dropout, he could absolutely never acknowledge as an Academy City esper.

"…Takitsubo has *always* had a rare 'nature'?" confirmed Hamazura, his voice shaking.

Yes.

*   *   *

"Are you saying you knew even before she went into the Curriculum? That no matter how hard you work, or how hard you study, the ones who are gonna succeed will succeed, and the ones who are gonna fail will fail?"

It was an answer more horrifying than hell.

Obviously, Academy City had a system—it was called the System Scan. It investigated an esper's aptitude using various methods, seeing what their current level was, the type of their ability, whether they'd grow quickly or slowly, things like that.

But that was only supposed to be a rough yardstick. It was believed that even students called Level Zero or Level One would grow if they worked hard enough. That was why they *could* work hard. Because they'd be rewarded one day. Because they'd bloom one day. They only wished for that.

And yet.

Wasn't a person who could work hard to go from a Level Zero to a Level Five simply established as someone who could have become a Level Five from the start? Did a person's nature, sleeping inside them, since before ever studying or enrolling, decide everything? Was the legend that you could make up for talent with hard work just a story to let them dance at their predetermined upper limits?

In that case.

Was there any hope for someone who was determined to be a Level Zero at birth?

"...You know, I always thought it was strange," said Shizuri Mugino thoughtfully. "I've taken a peek at the project related to number three. She was deceived in her childhood, and the DNA map she provided was used as the basis for a project to mass-produce somatic-cell clones for military use...But when you think about it rationally, the timing didn't make sense. Number three supposedly took time to grow from a Level One to a Level Five. Meaning she wasn't a Level Five yet when she provided her DNA mapping."

The term *military clone* was shocking, too, but Hamazura decided it wasn't impossible with Academy City's technology. "Wait, so you mean…The scientists knew from the start? They knew she'd eventually become a Level Five, so they took action before the value of her DNA mapping went up…?"

In response, the woman in the suit heaved a sigh inside her helmet. "Well, even the Parameter List brings evils with it. For example, a Level Five's DNA patent or biotic resources carry extraordinary value, but securing them costs a significant amount of capital. However, you can obtain it from a Level One with the possibility of becoming a Level Five in the future on a strict budget. Every time a fragmentary list gets leaked, it causes an issue where blood is shed behind the scenes from people trying to get rich quick."

"…"

"Still, though, I think it's positive on the whole. Integrating people who would never grow from the beginning into complicated Curricula would be a waste of time, money, and equipment—everything. It's far more effective to funnel what would be wasted into talented espers."

"You…bitch…!!"

It was not Hamazura who shouted, but Mugino.

She was furious, and Takitsubo tried to hold her back. Seeing that, the military woman spoke in an amused voice. "My, this isn't like you at all. After your battles, have you started to empathize with the feelings of the weak?"

"Shut up!!" screamed Mugino, anger in her eye. "That means it's all your fault Hamazura fell into a place like this!! Takitsubo and I chose this path for ourselves. The road and the environment were both complicated, and I don't think we'll be able to correct our course just by solving one problem. But the only thing supporting Hamazura was him being powerless! Because you all decided that for yourselves and cut corners on his Curriculum!! Sure, maybe he couldn't have become a Level Five. Maybe he would have stopped part of the way there. But if you'd actually given him an equal opportunity, he would have had the chance to grow a little, at least!! And if you had, if you had done that…!!"

…Shiage Hamazura may have never even joined Skill-Out.

He might not have ever needed to be dragged into Item, further into the depths of the darkness.

Maybe he would never have needed to be on the run from Academy City—maybe he could have led a totally normal student life.

…He might have had that boring but blessed world that nobody here was able to grasp, as if it was natural.

"It's fine," said Hamazura to Mugino, shaking her head. He was happy remembering that she'd gotten seriously angry for him in this situation. "We are Item. I don't regret that. So it's fine."

Mugino, then, was the one to avert her face, unable to stand it any longer.

Without knowing what kind of expression he was making right now, he changed the topic. "More importantly, you said something interesting."

While confirming the conditions inside his mind.

"Parameter List. Meaning there's an actual file? Its existence would be enough to plunge all the students living in Academy City into despair and powerlessness. I don't know what you and the other leaders are trying to do, but I'm sure you don't want to risk the City's functions stopping. Meaning we still have room for negotiation."

"Unconfirmed intel aside, do you think you'd have a chance to get the real thing? It's set up so that students like you, especially, will never be able to touch it. And above all…"

Clack-clack, came numerous metallic noises.

The sound of the people in white combat uniforms surrounding them aiming their rifle muzzles.

"Have you forgotten? Your life, at the very least, will end here."

Mugino's Meltdown wasn't usable.

Takitsubo's Ability Stalker didn't have an effect on anyone except espers.

Hamazura couldn't clean up a professional combat group of ten all at once by himself, either.

And…

"I think you're the one forgetting about something."

"?"

"Maybe you stop seeing it when you live in a filthy world like that. But this spot I'm standing in now isn't Academy City. It's not the same cruel stage. And I'm just a regular Level Zero. I never had any special powers that would let me fight my way out of this huge war by myself."

"..."

Perhaps feeling like she didn't need to listen any further, the woman in the suit raised her arm slightly.

That was all.

The men in white put their fingers on their triggers in unison.

Baaaaang!!

A sharp, splitting gunshot rang out across the white snowfield.

There was a red color, sullying the pure-white landscape.

Hamazura hadn't closed his eyes.

Because he hadn't needed to.

"Wha...?"

The shocked voice came from the helmeted woman in the suit. And no one could blame her—Hamazura wasn't the one who had fallen with the gunshot. Nor had it been Takitsubo or Mugino. It had been several of the ten soldiers surrounding them.

At the same time, hidden behind the clusters of trees in the woods and past the bulges of hills, encircling the men surrounding Hamazura and the others at an even wider circle, were about thirty men and women pointing assault rifles their way. They were Russians, but they didn't appear to be regular soldiers. Their clothing was civilian, and their rifles were somewhat battered, giving them a strange sense of regular usage.

"You alive, Hamazura?!"

Shouting that in Japanese was Digurv.

Next to him, also gripping a rifle, was Grickin, who tsked and said, "You told us to run away, but in the end, everyone came flying back, saying they couldn't abandon you!! Anyway, are those guys friends of the ones trying to set up the Steam Dispenser?!"

"…Not quite, but thanks. We cheated death thanks to all of you."

Hamazura slowly exhaled and relaxed himself.

He'd been spotting shadows in the scenery while they were talking to the helmeted woman. After that, he had to drag out the conversation until they finished getting into position.

"…How?"

The woman appeared sincerely confused.

"The state of the war between Academy City and the Russian military has been overwhelmingly one-sided the entire time. After all that, how could we possibly have been placed in a predicament this easily…?"

"Academy City was only in an advantageous position during the war because of its large-scale coordination and their powerful support of one another…Doesn't mean everyone's invincible—especially not independent teams running around by themselves like you guys."

Hamazura forced his still-stiff cheek muscles to move to create a smile.

"You know I'm right. If every single one of you was actually invincible, Takitsubo and I wouldn't ever have escaped Academy City to begin with."

"Do you think you've won?" spat the woman, smiling scornfully at them. She didn't seem to care about her fallen colleagues. "The system that's been monitoring you all until now is still running. Reinforcements will be here soon. Your situation won't change."

"Probably…So we'll just have to finish things before that."

After saying that, Hamazura spoke to the people from the settlement.

"Digurv, Grickin. You guys tie up the ones in the white combat uniforms and watch them to make sure they don't try anything funny."

And then he turned his head toward Item.

"Mugino, you hold Takitsubo back. I'm about to do something a little stimulating."

"What…?" began the helmeted woman in the suit, but Hamazura didn't answer her.

Instead, he immediately pulled out his gun and shot her in the right elbow and right knee.

Bang-bang!! Two dry gunshots rang out, and the woman in the suit let out a long scream. Hamazura's expression didn't change. He grabbed her suit collar in both hands, then started through the snow, dragging her behind him.

"...There's a little cave about a hundred meters up. We'll continue things there."

His voice was utterly calm, with no emotion in it whatsoever.

"An Academy City interception team will get here soon. I've gotta get our negotiation tool ready before then. And I'm willing to do whatever it takes to get it. I'm after the Parameter List. It can be the real thing printed on paper or a password for getting to the data on the Internet. Anyway, you're telling me everything you know. I'll make it so your mouth will be open before you even realize it's happening."

"Hee-hee..."

"Humans sure are scary, huh?" he said softly, bringing his mouth next to her helmet so that Takitsubo and Mugino couldn't hear. With an utterly flat voice. "If they can make the excuse that they're protecting someone precious, they can do the most brutal things. That's how it seems to me. And you're about to see how cruel humans can *really* be."

Accelerator lay atop a hill.

Neither Last Order nor Misaka Worst was here. Only the white snow, stretching on as far as the eye could see. Accelerator had crashed into the unknown energy mass fired from the fortress eight thousand meters high, but even he didn't understand what had happened after that. The white wings had disappeared from his back, too. He decided, at least, that his being barely alive like this meant he was able to stop the destruction at the last moment.

He heard a loud noise.

A large transport helicopter with two rotors on it. The hunk of metal was slowly descending to a spot near Accelerator as he looked up into the sky as he was lying there. A sliding door opened, and out of it came several people who looked more like a disaster rescue team than soldiers, wearing baggy protective gear reminiscent of space suits. He could see them bringing down a stretcher attached to their belts.

Retrieval.

Accelerator remembered the time he'd crushed Amata Kihara on September 30. It was the same as back then. He'd come through a grand battle and had invited grand chaos. Instead of leaving it to them to deal with, he put himself in the custody of Academy City's underworld and taken on dirty jobs.

In the end, no matter how much he fought or how far he ran, even if he left Academy City and fled Japan, he couldn't escape this massive cycle. He knew he'd faintly realized this. More than his own environment and situation, those of the Sisters and Last Order were just way too severe. He doubted they could live an honest life without Academy City's support.

They picked up his exhausted body and put him on the stretcher. From above, they wound him in several layers of thick belts. Treating his body as though they were transporting a tool—no, a weapon, they loaded him into the giant helicopter.

He didn't resist.

With a tremendous shaking, the transport helicopter began to leave the surface.

Strapped in with belts, Accelerator muttered dimly, "What about the kids?"

"Different team."

Only a couple short words came back.

"Hmph," snorted Accelerator. "...Then promise me this. Don't ever give orders using that kid or the Sisters as a shield. And freeze the Third Season. Killing 'em, making 'em, doesn't matter. Never toy with their lives for your own convenience ever again."

" ... "

"Release everyone in the same circumstances I was in, too. I won't allow you to use anything as a shield to push dirty jobs on people in the underworld. If I catch you doing it even once, I will not hesitate to turn against you. I will crush you as many times, as many *dozens* of times as I need to, as long as you keep up these atrocities."

"You don't seem to understand anything. Do you think you're in a position to make a deal?"

"No, you're the one who doesn't seem to get it."

One sentence.

As if sensing danger from it, the researcher in the protective suit put a hand to the side of Accelerator's neck. His ability worked on proxy calculations from the Misaka network. He was trying to check the switch on the electrode he needed to access the network.

However.

That mindset, of all things, was what Accelerator took advantage of.

The moment the researcher's fingertips touched the switch, Accelerator, still strapped in with belts, swung his neck. As a result, the finger on the switch slid across it, sliding it to its maximum setting.

His power returned.

The black belts holding his body down instantly flew off. The man in the protective suit was blown to the helicopter wall, and thick cracks formed in the fitted reinforced-glass window. His nearby colleagues got up in a panic, but it was too late.

"This isn't a negotiation, or a proposal, or a deal, or a plea, or an agreement, or a compromise, or a surrender."

Accelerator's arm touched the transport helicopter's wall.

Like paper ripping, the military-steel wall began to be easily destroyed. An incredibly chilly wind blew in, but the people in the protective suits couldn't pay attention to that. The terror of never knowing when the helicopter would plummet began to dominate the craft.

Amid it all, the king of monsters ruling over that fear simply said:

*   *   *

"This is my triumphant homecoming, you shitheads."

Using one finger to toy with the transport helicopter's minimum aerodynamic balance, wearing a smile that seemed to split his face in two, Accelerator added:

"And to start, I'll go rescue that kid and Misaka Worst."

Fiamma of the Right, hand trembling, opened the metal door from the inside.

Because of the damage gnawing away at his whole body, he couldn't even get up. He rolled outside the escape container.

He was on top of a low mountain.

The Star of Bethlehem he'd built up was nowhere to be found. The skies had returned to their original color, too. And he could no longer hear that constant nearby drumfire. A silent white. As he stared across the Russian scenery expanding out from the escape container, Fiamma came to a vague answer.

It was all over.

He didn't know what would become of the world after this. He knew he'd picked the best option at the moment. And now that it had been turned away, this world would be continuing its slide down the slope even now. How far would it fall? Or would it veer onto a different course as it fell? He was unable to make any predictions.

That man had instructed him to live in a world like this.

It hadn't been mere lip service. The man had gone through with it, full force, even giving his only chance to escape to a stranger.

Then now's when you start getting out there and seeing everything you can.

Those final words rang keenly in his ears. And so Fiamma, without going straight down into the snow, lay atop the ground like this, his objective lost. Needless to say, his path from here on would be a rocky one. He'd thrown the world into chaos, and they'd chase him down as the criminal who caused a war. He wouldn't have the

Roman or Russian Churches' cooperation. God's Right Seat was no more. He'd lost the Soul Arm that remotely controlled Index. His arm may have held a special power, but in a restricted situation, if he fought endlessly appearing enemies, it would eventually run out of steam. In this world of the victors, Fiamma would be treated as the one stain remaining.

A life on the run would be like something that whittled away at the surface of his body.

In such a swamp, he doubted he would find what that man had told him about.

"..."

But for some reason, Fiamma couldn't easily give up the possibility that another had risked his life to leave to him. At the time, that man had certainly seen something Fiamma couldn't. He hesitated to simply discard it without learning what it was.

He would determine where he was going once he started going, he decided.

Everything lost to him, Fiamma slowly put energy into his whole body once more, with his own feet. Wobbling, he stood up—and took his first step.

And then it happened.

Boom!!

Suddenly, Fiamma's right arm was cut off at the shoulder.

He hadn't been able to sense any sorcery activating, or any signs of something similar during the strike. The attack had fired from behind him and brutally sheared his limb off. His right arm, the symbol of his power. Having lost it, Fiamma, scattering red blood onto the white snow, screamed.

Holding the wound with his other hand, he turned around.

There was a strange sorcerer.

Silvery hair, colorless, reaching to his waist. A clean-cut face betraying no expression. Clothing consisting only of a green operating gown in this terrible cold. A strange atmosphere that made him look both male and female, both adult and child, both saint and sinner.

He knew him.

Fiamma of the Right knew this sorcerer.

However.

"...Aleister Crowley...?"

"As I thought, you correctly recognized me even without the vessel. By using a life-support system to mechanically create life force itself, the foundation of mana, I escaped all investigations in the past—but in this state, I suppose it only natural I would not be able to receive its blessings."

"You—I see—but that logic creates a contradiction. It doesn't explain why you're here."

"I assure you, there is nothing strange about this."

The sorcerer who should rightly have been in a windowless building in the heart of Academy City answered the question as though it were a matter of course.

"The very existence of Anna Sprengel, window to the Secret Chiefs and collaborator in the Golden society's establishment, was pronounced dubious...I, too, am one who functioned as a window to Aiwass—a theory of the Secret Chiefs'. Frankly, I doubt Aiwass would undertake such a grandiose, overly straightforward duty as giving permission for the establishment of sorcerer's societies around the world, and in the first place, there is no need to get such permission, but well, it is likely of the same essence as the being of which Anna spoke. Which means there is nothing mysterious about having exceeded the domain describable with only zeroes and ones."

Aleister Crowley, even now, existed in the center of Academy City.

But at the same time, Aleister Crowley, even now, existed before Fiamma.

There weren't multiple clones of him.

He could simply exist in multiple locations in his one body.

A phenomenon that caused fundamental concepts of enumerability to collapse; but that itself was the highest domain. In the first place, the Sephirothic Tree provided an explanation to the spiritual world using various words and numbers, but when it came to upper organizations beyond a certain point, they were purposely left out as something inexplicable with words.

Would one who stepped into that domain arrive at one of those upper organizations? Or would arriving at that upper organization cause it to be transformed into that domain?

Either way, Crowley was in a place in a different dimension.

In an even higher place than Fiamma, who had declared he had the power to save everyone in the world and yet was no more than one of the countable beings in this world.

"...Why?" murmured Fiamma. "I couldn't do it. Even though I should have had the power to save the world, just as Jesus Christ did. And I couldn't do that."

"That was no more than a matter of how you used your power, not its quality or quantity," said Aleister Crowley in a bored-sounding tone. "In my humble opinion, the age of Crossist spells ended with the completion of the *Book of the Law*. I actually think you made it quite far. Including your keen eye for the *kami-jo*, the god above. Had you decided to format not with the rules of a Crossist-domination world—the Age of Osiris—and instead with the Age of Horus after that, you may have set your sights on a place similar to me."

He who created supernatural powers using science.

He who constructed angels based on their gathering.

Fiamma of the Right, who controlled Michael, knew what that meant. Producing an angel wasn't merely creating a new form of life. A symbol of an aspect comprising the world—creating *that* with human hands equated to artificially interfering with the very system underlying this world.

The deed of attempting to embed a human-created cog into the mechanisms God had created, to reassemble a music box into a time bomb.

The inspiration to not only accept the occult but to try to ram precision instruments in it.

The thought processes to guide anything from the old age to the gallows just by thinking about it.

"...Is Aiwass such an attractive being?" asked Fiamma. "An angel that neither the Bible nor theology can explain. And a symbol of an aspect outside God's hands in a world He created—the clue to tearing down the fate He assigned...You didn't want the *Book of the Law*. You wanted the aberrant angel itself that initiated you in its ways."

Aleister neither confirmed nor denied it.

"Well, originally, this was not the stage in which I should have appeared," spoke the sorcerer called the most terrible in the world. "You may not understand the value in things, but you got a little too deeply involved with that right hand. You should have just recognized it as something that simply erased any strange powers, but you likely glimpsed what lies within it. I could not rightly leave you. Loath though I may be to admit it, you've forced my hand."

"What lies within...?"

"And this ending, as well. To think it would fall from my hands. Thanks to that, I need to take quite the detour...Ah, I may be feeling a natural anger as a living creature."

"..."

Fiamma's eyebrow twitched slightly.

He'd just remembered the thing that had flowed out when he'd cut off that boy's right arm.

"What was that?"

"I think you know," came the dismissive response. "Putting aside the fact that the formatting at the core of your actions was too old, it was very similar to my own plan. The idea to prepare a temple filled with aberrant forces, scour that right arm's power within it, and with that power, readjust the depth of the very phases, resulting in a transformation of the world. How is it different from the miniature world in which a certain kind of power called Academy City is sealed? You need only realign your view of your own actions to a different standpoint. That would have been all it took for you to understand that power's true essence...Of course, had you succeeded, you may have reached your objective a step even before me."

And that was why Aleister had come here.

"That parchment. A badly made thing, consolidated by Russian Catholic hands, but it being analyzed by anti-sorcerer institutions such as the English Church would have been a problem as well. I had my teams act in a somewhat gaudy manner this time, but in the end, thankfully, we recovered it...But that alone isn't enough. Do you understand what I'm trying to say?"

Fiamma was no fool. It was so Aleister could quash any possibility of Fiamma piecing together Aleister's plans from the unsuccessful incident he'd caused. Because of that, he couldn't even transfer custody to a sorcery faction. At this time, Fiamma had gotten the closest to the truth of this world.

"I see." Only one arm left, Fiamma of the Right still slowly shook his head. "...But none of that matters anymore."

Strangely, his face was drained of the strange passion that had followed him up until that moment.

As if something he possessed had slipped out of him.

"When I look at your face, I can feel how empty everything I've done is. I've probably made the same face myself. A face nobody who would really save the world would ever make...At that time, in that place, he stood in a spot where nobody could catch him."

Fiamma felt like he understood a little of what he'd lacked.

And so he took his left hand, which was covering his wound to hold back the blood loss, and of his own will removed it. At the same time, there was a loud *boom!!* The spurting blood outlined a giant, transparent arm. His third arm. A power he could no longer control of his own volition—but for a little while, he could still fight.

"I doubt that will work."

Aleister Crowley didn't even take a stance. He moved the fingers on a hand, slowly grabbing something invisible. During his pantomiming motion, Fiamma sensed something strange. It felt like a staff, one that couldn't possibly exist, had revealed itself. No—he was right. It didn't exist in the real world. Despite that, due to unclassified information such as mood and atmosphere, it was as though he was seeing an illusion—in color, even: silver.

The Blasting Rod.

The rod from an old sorcerer's tale where Crowley, once referred to as the ultimate evil, had decided to ask his teacher for direction out of pure respect.

"It was never about whether it would work," Fiamma stated quietly.

Aleister would probably never understand, even given a hundred years.

If true feelings of wanting to save others took precedence, then obviously one's chance at winning had to be relegated.

Then now's when you start getting out there and seeing everything you can.

Someone who could answer with that, without hesitation, to an enemy who had said they didn't understand how big the world was, probably knew a lot more than he did. Much more that wasn't recorded even in the original copies of grimoires. Fiamma wasn't even sure he'd grasped a glimpse of it, but because of that, he thought this:

He couldn't let Aleister crush that underfoot.

Even if it meant confronting a true monster.

That man had risked his life to save the world—and he couldn't let Aleister trample on that anymore.

The duel's outcome was clear as day.

Two figures collided, and one fell down the mountain's sloped surface.

Silence once again returned to the white Russian landscape.

The victor cast a single glance down the slope before saying, while melting his body into the air, "…The fact that you sought to explain the right hand and the Imagine Breaker and the *kamijou*—god's purification—with your petty Crossist ideas—*that* was your failure."

And then, in faraway London, someone was smiling.

"We detected something!! Only for about seven hundred seconds, but this wavelength is unmistakable. It belongs to the sorcerer Aleister Crowley!!"

St. George's Cathedral.

As she received the report from an English Puritan Sister, the Archbishop, Laura Stuart, gave a lip-twisting smile.

A man who should have been dead.

A sorcerer who was supposed to have been buried by English Puritan assassins.

There had been an official report that he'd died over sixty years ago, but experts on Crowley continued to exist so that they could deal with the sorcerer's society that named itself his successor—and the theories that he himself might still be alive. And now, an individually set-up Soul Arm for searching had just given them an unexpected result.

Of course.

For Laura Stuart, that "unexpected result" was no more than how people thought the universe was born—theories existed, but nobody had ever found a way to prove it.

The search spell, which used farsightedness, was nearly useless, only showing a blurred outline of the figure that appeared. The target seemed to be conversing with someone, but they couldn't make out the details, either.

Nevertheless, that paltry amount of information made Laura confident.

His features had changed quite a bit.

And he may have well have been using some sort of perception-blocking method all this time.

However.

...I knew it. He is alive.

Laura had never believed that his existence had truly disappeared.

Certainly, after World War III, the ones who would gain the most would be the victors: Academy City. After this, the scales of the sorcery-science power balance would unavoidably tip far toward science. The Roman and Russian Churches' power would weaken, and though the English Church had won the war, they were no more than one of the *three* largest denominations of Crossism. Academy City, however, was the *single* leader of the science side. It was a simple matter of power distribution. The victors' apportionment of world control would, no matter how one looked at it, be in favor of Academy City.

But it wouldn't end in a place like this.

If Academy City's general board chairperson was who Laura estimated he was, it then gave her the right to kill Crowley. And traditionally, targets of witch-hunting would forfeit their assets to the Church.

In other words.

There was still a chance to steal everything from the greatest winners of the war: Academy City and the science side.

Obviously, even if her guess was right, he wouldn't roll over for her. She couldn't deny the chance a fourth war would happen, either. But those things didn't matter. As long as there was a chance, as long as there was hope for putting the whole world at their fingertips, none of that mattered a bit.

The Royals had been concerned that it didn't matter whether Academy City or the Roman Church won World War III—the United Kingdom would be forced to walk a path of decline. Enough so that the second princess, for example, had caused a coup.

Laura Stuart's answer to that was this:

They could just pluck from the victors.

Pluck away everything they had.

After all, it was the English Church's special right as an anti-sorcerer organization to put the sorcerer Aleister Crowley to death and keep his dangerous fortunes for themselves.

Had the Roman Church won, things would have moved toward a decisive expansion of the Crossist world as well as the magic side's domination of the world, so for her, despite being an English Puritan—a faction of Crossism—she'd no longer be able to come up with a pretext. Or at least, she wouldn't be able to use an inquisition to snatch everything away.

That was why she needed Academy City.

And the situation had taken a delightful turn for the better.

"...Now then, Chairperson Aleister—it is the hour when things truly grow interesting."

Heh-heh, came a soft chuckle.

Atop an Academy City building, the being called Aiwass was looking at its hands and laughing, distinctly and amusedly.

When Accelerator had interfered with Last Order's mind, the power holding Aiwass's existence here had been greatly reduced. Soon, Aiwass would withdraw for a time from the "surface." Nevertheless, Aiwass was cheerful.

"...You seem to be enjoying yourself."

It heard a voice. A girl's.

Hyouka Kazakiri.

The light in her eyes, behind her glasses, was a sharp one, unusual for the constantly afraid girl.

"I am delighted," said Aiwass, moving its hands out slightly. "More precisely, I am happy this delightful time seems like it will continue. With *that* method, it would have ended in the blink of an eye. As though not very many dominoes were lined up before someone flicked the first. In order to enjoy this situation, I should retreat into the depths for a time. Livestock is best eaten once it's fattened."

"All this for that?"

"Why, yes. Whether or not I had appeared, the command tower would not have lasted long. It didn't have the strength to line up the dominoes. Thus, to grant the necessary strength, I provided a hint... And he did well. This method was not in my elimination, but in the shift to a different domain. Still, it was a very good job on his part to do this much."

Whether it saw value and interest or not.

That was the only condition this being, who could instantly destroy this star if it was unnecessary, ever acted on.

"I think you should learn more about what humans are."

"?"

"It's strange that you never knew from the start. After all, it's their power that supports our bodies. They have so much possibility sleeping in them that they can give us form. Needless to say, humans are incredibly strong creatures...If you make light of them, you'll find your heart pierced before you know it."

"What are you saying?" answered Aiwass, looking back at Kazakiri but not hiding its excitement. "If a frail human could truly do something like that...That would be so incredibly fascinating, don't you think?"

Mikoto Misaka arrived on the shore.

But it was a very different shore than Japan's bathing beaches. It was technically a small fishing port, but she didn't know if it was running at the moment. After all, the sea had been completely covered in white ice before. The water was flowing.

The VTOL hadn't had enough fuel, so she'd been forced to land on the surface.

She'd boarded a high-speed freight train, but even then, she'd been definitively late.

She'd gone in the direction of the floating fortress, and kept going, and kept going, and kept going, but what she'd run into was this fishing port.

Possibly because of the evacuation warning from when the fortress was falling, nobody was around. The roads nearby were awfully frozen; maybe after the tsunami had hit, the chill had frozen the water.

She hadn't found a trace of anything that might provide a clue about the boy.

Looking around at a loss, Mikoto eventually picked up a large stick. From a concrete embankment, she reached out with the stick and stirred around the seawater, its surface covered in ice like a soda at a café.

The tip of the stick caught onto some kind of small plastic clump.

The Sister next to her asked her what it was.
Mikoto couldn't answer.
Exactly *because* she'd seen it before.

Its string torn apart by some strong force, it was a Croaker cell phone strap.
Something they'd gotten together on August 30.

DECLARATION OF THE END OF HOSTILITIES

We must not allow this fruitless war to continue any longer.

After a careful examination of Academy City's proposed conditions, we have agreed to hold talks. The details will be worked out then, but we hereby declare that it will not result in any disadvantage for Russia.

Before, we failed to listen to the words of the people and made an irreversible choice based on the opinions of a few. You all likely sense much more strongly how much tragedy this carried with it. I do not have the words to vindicate this historical failing.

The least we are able to do is put an end to this abnormal state of affairs as soon as possible and restore the world so that it can enjoy peace, as is its right.

After everything has ended, we will accept any punishment.

But until then, we ask that you grant us some measure of grace.

Some may not be convinced by this ending. The act of laying down our arms may not sit right with you. But we ask that you think with a clear mind—what was this war for? If this was a battle to protect our families, our friends, our spouses, and our loved ones, then this is precisely the moment we can say we've done it. Any further combat action would do no less than bring us farther away from that.

What made us realize that fact was the exploits of everyone on the battlefield.

During the supernatural disasters that occurred at the end of the war, you all made a far more correct choice than us in providing a helping hand to enemy and ally alike. We are confident that you will accept this ending.

At this time, we announce an end to all combat operations.

And we pray that the choice you have obtained will be written in the history books of a future peaceful world as the correct one.

October 30
        Klans R. Tzarskij, Patriarch of the Russian Catholic Church

He'd been beaten to a pulp.

His right arm had been severed.

Even exposed to the air's slicing chill, he could no longer move a finger. He could feel the blizzard slowly burying him.

But then...

He heard footsteps coming through the snow.

A moment later, figures appeared in his upturned view. No, they hadn't approached by walking—they'd appeared in a more unnatural fashion, as though they'd shown up exactly when he'd perceived them.

They were an odd pair.

One was a blond woman. She had goggles, pushed up onto her forehead, and wore a work apron over a deep-colored jacket and pair of pants made of a thick, practical fabric. Her appearance was sloppy, but he could sense refinement in her motions. She gave the impression of a waiting maid from Britain.

The other one was a blond man. Over his light-blue shirt, he had on a beige vest.

He was in no place to comment on others, but those were not

clothes that would allow movement in this bitter cold. And yet, they never even rubbed their hands together for warmth.

The woman spoke.

"Looks like he's still breathing, at least."

"A result of his sheer strength, no doubt. He had no reason to hold back in that situation," answered the man before looking at his fallen face. "Anyway, I'm sure you'd rather this not end with such a complete beatdown. We're almost at the end of our ropes ourselves, at least…We can promise you housing and safety for the time being. In exchange, we want you to tell us everything you heard. Because we may be able to read past the Age of Osiris you were in and into the Age of Horus—of Crowley—that comes after."

"Who…are you…?" Fiamma asked. His voice was ragged.

"Ollerus." The answer was short, everything compressed into that one word. "A pitiful sorcerer who should have become a magic god—only to have that position stolen by the one-eyed Othinus."

AFTERWORD

To those of you who purchased one book at a time, hello again.

To those of you who purchased all twenty-three volumes at once, it's nice to meet you.

I'm Kazuma Kamachi.

This book is Volume 22. And with it, the God's Right Seat arc comes to an end for the present. It started with a mention of Vento around Volume 11, so it's been going for about ten volumes just in the main novels, give or take.

This is a good opportunity, so I'd like to touch on each of the three protagonists.

Regarding Touma Kamijou.

He is a "relative" character, through and through. Without any sorcerers or espers with special powers around him, even the existence of his ability to cancel them out will never be seen. Even when beliefs clash with beliefs, in most cases, he doesn't mount the attack himself—it's presented in a way where he responds to what the opponent has to say. If someone without any special power, who had straightforward, honest beliefs, had come at him with fists clenched, Kamijou would have lost without a doubt...Of course, there may not be any reason to fight someone like that in the first place.

If Shiage Hamazura, as he currently is now that he's grown

somewhat, beat Kamijou in a regular brawl, the power balance between the three protagonists would turn into a triangular struggle. That might be interesting— What do you think?

Some readers may feel that something was different about Kamijou in this volume. However, this was mostly the enemy being out of this world rather than Kamijou having grown. He seems more amazing now that he can deal with their amazing powers, which elevates his position in a relative sense.

At his core, he is a character whose position is unknown.

If he heard a pet cat had gotten out, he'd put 100 percent into finding it, and if a crisis threatened the world, he'd put 100 percent into stopping it. He's earnest about everything, and yet, depending on the essence of the incident, the direction of that earnestness changes completely, making him a strange person, I think.

And in this series, several characters appear whom you could call Kamijou's polar opposites. This changes based on what part of Touma Kamijou they cut down, but that just means Kamijou has that many facets to his character.

I envision the world of *A Certain Magical Index* not as an overarching storyline wherein many characters appear, but something where stories occur around the characters set up as the protagonists (with SS2 being the most prominent exception). For each of the protagonists, stories happen with them that make that protagonist stand out the most. But with Kamijou, it feels like he can do anything, from going through wars with cannonballs firing all over the place to cooking battles with a bubbling Chinese hot pot...It's not about having many and varied talents but going forward without caring that he's an amateur, and that probably makes him easy to write as the protagonist of a story. If he was some kind of expert, on the other hand, I'd have to set up some sort of deep and complex circumstances for him to challenge anything outside his field.

Regarding Accelerator.

He's depicted in the main series as a dark hero, but from another angle, he has a saintlike quality to him. It's the type of thing where someone who had committed a so-called grave sin walks a path of suffering to atone for it.

As proof of overcoming those trials, his wing color changes dramatically...That scene was something I'd wanted to do for a long time.

What Accelerator wants, deep down, is not a lover but a family. But he's never known a family, so while he treats Last Order like a parent would (even without it being clear whether it's like a father or a mother), he allows Yoshikawa and Yomikawa to treat him as a child (notably in Volume 15, in the scene when Yomikawa takes away his gun), so he's always been in something of a contradictory position.

His calling himself a villain was both a symbol of his past and a way to give himself a convenient way out. Now that he's destroyed his own complex over good and evil in Volume 22, Accelerator will probably need to face his "family" without any more excuses.

Regarding Shiage Hamazura.

In this war, Touma Kamijou and Accelerator were sticking to the irregular portions, so I gave him a role that would make the reader feel the smell of war a bit more.

His complex is, though maybe it doesn't need to be said, his grades in school—the scarlet letter of the Level Zero. However, now that he's realized the Curriculum and System Scan results are nothing more than guidelines given by Academy City's leadership to guide children's futures at the whims of adults, he's broken the chains binding his own mind and succeeded in rescuing an ally who was also chained down by her elite Level Five rank.

He doesn't stick mainly to the sorcery side or the science side—he's on the Hamazura side—but in the latter part of the story, he encounters things quite close to the central core of everything. The specific factors refined using Level Fives, for example. Dark Matter is a very unique example and is unverifiable, but with Accelerator and Railgun as well, I think it's really neat to view things from the perspective of industry in addition to simple biotic resources. What about you?

I think that if you apply this way of thinking, you'll understand the question of why number seven, who appeared in SS2, is very strong but only ranked seventh…And number five, who at a glance can't physically interfere with anything, which means her added value seems low, can get enormous results in fields like sports and medicine.

…Also, and this is incidental, but in terms of male-female relationships and their viewed worth, I think Hamazura has progressed the furthest. He's probably the only protagonist who could have given a real answer after that super-cutting line: "But you chose _____, didn't you?" I would have liked to give a certain spiky-haired boy the same question.

I'd like to thank my illustrator, Mr. Haimura, and my editor, Mr. Miki. This being the last part of the God's Right Seat arc, there were quite a few huge gimmicks, and I'm sure illustrating them was a monumental task. Thank you, truly, for putting up with my troubling instructions again.

And I'd like to thank all my readers. I could only unwrap the God's Right Seat arc this far because you were all supporting me. Thank you so much for supporting this environment where I can do whatever I want to such a degree.

Now then, as you close the pages here,
and as I pray you will open the pages again next time,
here and now, I lay down my pen.

Next up is the saved world!!